ME TOO

SHORT STORIES

An Anthology

Edited by
ELIZABETH ZELVIN

LEVEL
BEST BOOKS

First published by Level Best Books 2019

Copyright © 2019 by Elizabeth Zelvin

First Edition

ISBN: 978-1-947915-13-8

Cover and interior design: SRS

Level Best Books

www.levelbestbooks.com

To the millions of women and girls who have survived abuse
and to those who didn't survive

and to Liz's mother
an immigrant at the age of four
she entered law school in 1921
Liz learned to edit at her knee
she lived almost forever
and wrote her own epitaph:
"Twentieth-century feminist from start to finish"

Contents

Praise for Me Too Short Stories   ii

Introduction   iii

Never Again by Elizabeth Zelvin – *read*   1

Pentecost by Eve Fisher   17

The Call is Yours by Rona Bell   31

The Final Recall by Diana Catt *read*   43

A Measured Death by Julia Pomeroy *read*   61

Miss Evelyn Nesbit Presents by Ana Brazil   82

Stepping on Snakes by Madeline McEwen   96

Women Who Love Dogs by Dayle A. Dermatis   111

Jewel's Hell by Lynn Hesse   126

Banshee Scream by Gin Gannon   139

No Outlet by V. S. Kemanis *read*   152

A Dog's Life by Ann Rawson   166

Subterfuge by Julia Buckley   189

The Taste of Collards by C. C. Guthrie   208

Chrissie by Carole Sojka   221

Discussion Questions   230

About the Editor   242

Praise for Me Too Short Stories

"This anthology is a treasure. Empowering, inspirational, and sometimes wickedly funny. Timely fiction like this provides a special kind of justice—giving not only insight and empathy but a new strength to voices that must be heard." - Hank Phillippi Ryan, nationally bestselling author of *Trust Me* and *The Murder List*

"Elizabeth Zelvin has put together a strong collection that reminds us—as if we ever need reminding—how the daily lives of women can be affected by the conduct of calculating or even careless men. The characters in these stories will challenge, surprise, and inspire you." - Alafair Burke, *New York Times* bestselling author of *The Better Sister*

"A soul-satisfying anthology of justice and revenge, expertly edited by Elizabeth Zelvin. Each story is a standout in its own way. If the deepest truths are revealed through fiction, then this anthology goes further, reflecting our own lives back and showing us how to live them just a bit better." - Jenny Milchman, *USA Today* bestselling author of *Cover of Snow* and *Wicked River*

Introduction

by Elizabeth Zelvin

A girl who's been abused since early childhood has finally had enough. A mother too poor to feed her kids anything but collard greens and black-eyed peas becomes a lioness when her cubs are threatened. A little girl in 1950s Cape Town, savvy because she has brothers, loses her best friend by trying to warn her about the stranger on the other side of the playground fence. An eleven-year-old, traveling alone on a cross-country red-eye, is confused—What *does* the man in the next seat have under his cowboy hat?—but resilient enough to get even in the morning. A banshee metes out justice when the law can't, quoting the Hippocratic Oath—*first do no harm*—to a plastic surgeon who thinks he's gotten away with murder. Is it a horror story if you're rooting for the banshee?

These are a few of the protagonists you'll meet in *Me Too Short Stories*. One is a Lutheran minister, one an unwilling prostitute, another a neurobiologist in a cutting-edge research lab. And then there's the notorious "girl on the red velvet swing." What do they have in common? Your first guess would be anger, and yes, like many real women in the world we're living in, they are angry. Some want vengeance. A few of them kill when provoked beyond bearing or to protect those they love. But they are driven by other passions too, including the desire for justice, healing, and redemption. Some, perhaps, yearn for a lost innocence that can never be regained. But once justice or vengeance is achieved, and sometimes even when it's not, a grievously hurt and damaged woman may discover that old wounds can be healed and the past laid to rest.

Never Again

by Elizabeth Zelvin

"What I don't understand," Valerie's friend Helen's little sister said, "is how Santa gets into the house. We don't have a chimney. Do you, Valerie?"

"No," Valerie said, standing on tiptoes to hang a fragile glass ball high on a fragrant branch of Helen's family's Christmas tree.

They didn't have a real tree at Valerie's house, only a fake table model. Valerie's dad had once thrown it across the room in a rage, and that was the end of pretty but breakable ornaments in their house. The problem wasn't Santa getting into the house, but her dad coming into her room in the middle of the night. And he didn't come for milk and cookies, either.

She remembered her mom, strange and swollen as Valerie hugged her around the knees with the giant belly resting on her head, telling her Daddy would take care of her while Mommy went to the hospital to bring back a little brother for her to play with. Then she was alone with Daddy. Instead of tucking her in the way Mommy always did, he sat down on her bed, spread

1

his knees wide, and beckoned her to come close. When he told her to get down on her knees, she thought he wanted her to say her prayers. Then he pushed her head down between his thighs.

That was the first time. Stevie was ten now, so she must have been four years old. From the beginning, she tried to look out for Stevie, who was delicate and cried easily. Daddy didn't do it to him. But he beat Stevie a lot. He could knock Stevie across the room with his big thick hand. He didn't even need to make a fist. Once Stevie hit the wall and got a concussion, and their mom had to take him to the hospital and tell a pack of lies.

Mom was taking a lot of pills by then. She hid them inside the shoes in the back of her closet, but any fool could find them if they looked. Even when Stevie was a baby, half the time she forgot to change his diapers, and Valerie had to do it. Or she'd say she had to take a nap, and Valerie would give Stevie his bottle, bathe him, and put him to bed. Then she'd eat something that didn't need cooking, like bologna or fig newtons, so she wouldn't go to bed hungry. Later, Valerie made sure Stevie did his homework, checked his head for lice if the school had an outbreak, and signed his permission notes for field trips with Mom's name.

She signed her own consent form for sex education class. The teacher tried not to seem embarrassed, but Valerie could tell she was. She used mealy-mouthed words like "inappropriate touching." If it had never happened to you, you wouldn't know what the hell she was talking about. If it had, you would think, as Valerie did, that *she* didn't know what the hell she was talking about. Afterwards, she invited any kids who had "questions about the material" or "issues that troubled them" to

2

come and see her in her office. As if that was going to happen!

Once, when she was seven, Valerie tried to tell her mom what her dad was doing to her. The sex ed teacher talked about that: "Tell a trusted adult what's going on. You don't have to deal with this alone." Not that they taught sex education to kids that young. It wasn't *appropriate*, even though it happened to four-year-olds. Her mom slapped her for telling lies. She said her dad was a good man who worked hard to provide for them all, and she didn't want to hear another word against him out of Valerie's mouth ever again.

"Or maybe you'd rather not live under this roof, missy," she said.

For a second, that sounded like good news. But then Valerie realized her mom didn't mean she could leave, maybe go and live with Aunt Marge and Uncle Bob instead of home. Seven was old enough to get it when adults said one thing and meant another. Anyhow, her dad had already told her that if she told, he'd kill her. Sometimes he said he'd kill Stevie or her mom. He seemed to know which one she cared the most about, usually Stevie, whenever he said it. She wasn't sure if he meant it, but she couldn't take the chance.

When she was eleven, she discovered cutting. She would take razor blades from her dad's bathroom and score her arms. She'd watch the blood trickle down like raindrops on a window, one of those big glass windows at school on a rainy afternoon when nobody listened to the teacher. It felt like she was a million miles away. It was sort of like the way she felt with her dad. Except with him, there was a terrified, squeaking, helpless little girl part that couldn't get away, like a mouse with a cat's paw on its head, and then the other Valerie, cool and far away above it all, who didn't feel a thing. When she cut, there was a Valerie who felt everything and a Valerie who floated, dizzy and numb. And she controlled the feelings. She had the power, nobody else.

Lately she felt split in two most of the time. She even felt it in Helen's living room. Half of her felt peaceful, putting ornaments on this nice normal family's nice normal Christmas tree. The other half wanted to run screaming from the room. She would never be a nice normal girl like Helen. This house, this room, this Christmas tree smelling of the woods and sparkling with silver icicles and light—unbearable. Paradise, and she could never get in. Her parents had already ruined it.

As she helped Helen and her little sister place wooden crèche figures under the tree and ate a warm chocolate chip cookie that their mother had baked—baked!—she thought, *I'm never doing it to him again. It'll be my Christmas present to myself.*

* * *

When Frances was ten, she had two secrets. One was the preacher's son and what he did to her. The other was the box of chocolates hidden away in the toy chest beneath her baby quilt with her ratty old teddy bear, loved practically bald and ever vigilant, on top to guard it. Now the chocolates—and the boxes of Krispy Kremes and pizzas and Big Macs and jumbo onion blossoms from the diner—weren't a secret, even if she had them delivered after dark when Donald was drinking himself into a stupor and everyone else on their street was watching TV or down at the bingo hall. All that food had turned into rolls of fat. The whole town saw it every Sunday at church. She could hardly squeeze into a pew these days.

She had to walk to church, panting, wearing compression

stockings and leaning on a cane. It was one of Donald's little cruelties not to keep a car that she could get in and out of. His latest ride was a pickup too high for her to climb into. He always boasted that he'd had it customized. One time in church, the wife of the owner of the biggest garage in town told her that that model was supposed to have a running board on the passenger side. He must have had it removed. Donald never tired of telling her he could sooner boost an elephant onto a gilded stage at the circus than boost her into the cab of that pickup.

Her other secret was how Donald slapped and pinched her. Since his drinking had gotten so much worse, he even punched her, sometimes beat her with his belt or a hairbrush or anything handy. He always did it where her clothes would hide the bruises. She'd never dressed to show much flesh. She'd learned shame young, when the preacher had thundered on about how Eve had tempted Adam, and then his son had smirked and said he'd show her the serpent that lived down in the church basement. He said she probably knew all about it 'cause she was a daughter of Eve. She didn't know what he was talking about, but she was afraid not to go with him, because he was bigger than her and known to be a bully when his father wasn't around. And then he'd clapped one meaty hand over her mouth so she couldn't scream and hurt her really bad.

She still saw the son in church every Sunday. He hadn't gotten the call to become a preacher, but he was a deacon. So was Donald, who when he punched her said things like, "Sheesh, Fanny, what are you squealing about? You didn't feel that, did you? It's like punching a pillow."

There was no point in trying to tell anyone, any more than there'd been in telling her mom about what the preacher's son had done. Back then her mother had washed out her mouth with soap and told her she'd go to hell for lying about a good boy from a good family. Donald said nobody believed fat women anyhow. He said everybody knew fat women lied about their weight and what they ate, so of course no one believed a word they said about anything else.

She'd had a neighbor once, a thin neighbor, who'd become sort of a friend. Sitting over coffee at Ivy's kitchen table one morning, she tried to explain what it was like to be invisible. Because she was so fat, no one ever looked at her as if they wanted to do what the preacher's son had done. One thing about Donald, he didn't bother her much that way. His true love was the bottle. But the fat also blotted out Frances. Not Sheesh Fanny or Hey Fatso or an island of numb in a sea of blubber, but the real Frances that nobody knew. Sad Frances. Mad Frances. Frances who might want to scream or even crack a joke once in a while. She couldn't remember the last time she had laughed. And she never cried. She wouldn't give Donald the satisfaction.

Ivy didn't get it.

"But you're very visible!" she said.

"No," Frances said. "I'm conspicuous."

Ivy moved away soon after that, and Frances never tried again.

* * *

"Valerie!" Aunt Marge peered out the door at Valerie standing on the mat with snowflakes drifting down onto her shoulders. "What are you doing here? It's Christmas Eve! Is something wrong at home? Well, don't just stand there, dearie. Come in, come in. Wipe your feet and tell me all about it."

If only she could! But Valerie couldn't take the risk. Aunt Marge was Mom's sister, not Dad's, but the sisters used to joke about what a "good catch" he was. He was better looking than Uncle Bob, who sold insurance. It seemed insurance was less glamorous than what Valerie's dad did, stockbroking. They sounded equally boring to her. Then Uncle Bob had died, and it turned out he hadn't sold himself enough insurance, so Aunt Marge was permanently pissed off with him. And now that Mom had lost interest in everything, even getting dressed and going shopping at the mall, Aunt Marge was more on Dad's side than ever, calling him "you poor man," bringing casseroles over, and telling Mom she really ought to make an effort for the children's sake.

Aunt Marge fluttered around her, hanging up her coat, putting her hat and gloves on the radiator to dry, asking her if she'd eaten. What she had to say wouldn't get any easier, so she just said it.

"Aunt Marge, I'm not going back. I want to come and live with you."

"I don't understand, darling," Aunt Marge said. "What on earth do you mean?"

"What I said." Valerie set her jaw in the way her mother used to call "mulish" when she still noticed things. "I can't live there anymore. *Please* let me stay. I'll do housework, I'll be quiet as a mouse, I'll do whatever you say. I'll pay rent if you want. I can get a job after school."

Aunt Marge sat down on the sofa and patted the cushion next to her, saying nothing until Valerie sat down. She put her arm around Valerie. She smelled of lavender bath powder.

"Darling, you're a teenager, and all teenagers get mad at their

7

parents. Believe it or not, I was a teenager once myself. And I see it all the time at school." Aunt Marge was a school librarian, though not in Valerie's school. "It will blow over, I promise. And then you'll remember how you really feel about them."

"I know how I feel," Valerie said. "I won't go back. If you won't let me stay, I'll run away."

"Oh, dear. Have you really thought it through? Running away is harder than you think."

Valerie could tell that Aunt Marge didn't take her seriously. She was trying not to smile.

"At least tell me what the fight was about," she said.

"There was no fight," Valerie said. "Honestly, Aunt Marge. It's not like that."

"Then tell me who you're angry with," Aunt Marge said. "Mommy or Daddy?"

Don't talk about them in that babyish way, Valerie wanted to say. It made them sound so harmless. Maybe if she cooperated a little, Aunt Marge would be more inclined to let her stay.

"My dad, I guess. *Please* help me, Aunt Marge."

Aunt Marge reached out and stroked her hair.

"You know I love you, darling. If you'd explain what the problem is, I could help you."

"I *can't*," Valerie said.

* * *

One afternoon, Frances turned on the radio to give herself some company while she ironed Donald's shirts. A woman preacher was talking about Christmas—not about Baby Jesus, but about the holiday, how people thought about it, how they celebrated. At her own church, where the men ran everything and hypocrisy was a given, Frances automatically tuned out the sermon, even when it was a visiting preacher. But she liked the woman preacher's voice. So she listened.

"Do you want the perfect Christmas gift?" the woman preacher said. "Don't wait for someone else to get it for you. Give it to yourself. No one is going to read your mind or guess your deepest wishes. Waiting for someone else to meet your expectations is a recipe for disappointment."

It was a novel idea, and it made sense. Frances's whole life was a series of disappointments. Was the problem her expectations? She certainly didn't expect the perfect gift from Donald. Last Christmas he had bought her a new vacuum cleaner. But Frances knew that wasn't what the woman preacher was talking about. She was really saying, *Are you happy? If not, what are you doing about it?*

What *was* the perfect Christmas gift? What would Frances give herself if she could have anything she wanted? *Freedom!* The word tolled in her head louder than the loudest Sunday steeple bell. All of a sudden, it seemed simple. She already knew she couldn't leave him. She couldn't even get in the truck and drive to the nearest bus depot. It would be easier to kill him.

* * *

"Dammit, a family should be together at Christmas." Valerie's father looked around the dinner table. "Steven! Stop picking at your food. Sandy, why don't you teach that boy manners? Did Valerie tell you where she was going? Don't lie to me, son."

"Oh, Chet, for heaven's sake, leave him alone," Valerie's mother said. "It's Christmas Eve. Your son wouldn't lie, would you, Stevie?"

Stevie hunched his shoulders, shook his head, and took a mouthful of mashed potatoes so big they couldn't make him speak.

"Does anyone want dessert?" she asked. "Then finish up. As soon as I clear the table, I'll call her friends and see if she's visiting one of them."

"Home's not good enough for her?" he growled. "We'll see about that."

Snow was falling, and black ice had been reported on the roads. Every time one of them looked out, thinking this time Valerie might appear, they saw smooth white mounds blanketing lawns, roofs, and bushes, spears of ice drooping from eaves, multicolored lights festooning evergreens, and a soft indigo filling in every inch of air and shadow.

"She's not with any of her friends," Valerie's mother said. "I'm beginning to worry."

"You should have started worrying hours ago," Valerie's father said, "when she started acting independent. Try your sister."

"Why didn't I think of Marge?"

She dialed, oblivious to her husband's snort of contempt.

"Marge? Is Valerie with you? Oh, thank goodness! I was so worried! Why didn't you make her call? Hush, Chet, Marge is trying to tell me something. Let me speak to her."

"Quack quack quack," Chet said. "What is there to talk about? Tell Valerie to put her coat on. She's coming home right now. If you're going to be all night about it, I'm going to watch TV."

"Wait, Chet," Sandy said. "Marge says she wanted to stay."

"What do you mean, stay? That's ridiculous! It's Christmas Eve. She belongs at home."

"Oh, Chet, what harm can it do to let her stay overnight? I'll pick her up after breakfast."

"Like hell you will," Chet said. "I'll go after her myself right now. Do you want to teach her she gets rewarded for running away?"

"For heaven's sake, Chet, let her have her sleepover."

"Forget it, Sandy. I'm on my way."

* * *

She waited for the perfect moment to send him out on the Interstate, where he considered it his God-given right to speed, with a slow leak in two of his tires that wouldn't cause his brakes any trouble until he was cruising at eighty, steering with his knees and chugging from the bottle of gin she'd thoughtfully provided. God or the devil provided the conditions on Christmas Eve. Freezing rain earlier in the day had turned into a blinding snowstorm and a glassy road: black ice beneath a layer of deceptive beauty. She'd figured it out all by herself, too. The Internet was no help. You couldn't google "How to kill your husband." And "What would make a single car crash on the highway?" yielded answers useful only to mechanics—old cars—or computer hackers—new cars. But even she could loosen the little caps at the end of the air valves, and nice guys in three different auto forums who didn't know or care who Sheesh Honey was assured her it would work but not too fast.

How did she get him on the Interstate on Christmas Eve? Easy. His insatiable craving for drink never failed. On Christmas Eve, Donald had to have his special eggnog laced like a Victorian wedding dress with just the right bourbon, rum, and brandy. It was a tradition, the only sweet drink he touched all year, and he made gallons of it. He liked to say that the way he made it, there was precious little egg or nog in it and a helluva lotta booze. Only one liquor store carried all three of his special brands. That liquor store was in a mall five towns away. All she had to do was untwist the valves, dump out the last of all three kinds of liquor from last year, and act surprised. *She* couldn't run that errand. She couldn't drive the truck, remember?

* * *

The road was dark, and traffic was light. Valerie's dad set the heater to blast the windshield and the wipers to brush off the thickly falling snow. He paid no attention to the stranded motorists whose cars had spun out of control onto the median or the sides of the road. There were even a couple of pileups, surprising considering how few people were driving on Christmas Eve. Only incompetent fools had accidents. He had perfect control behind the wheel.

So Valerie thought she could waltz out any time she wanted, did she? His foot pressed harder on the gas pedal as irritation surged through him. Didn't she know by now that family is forever? If not, it was time to teach her another lesson.

He bared his teeth in an ugly smile. His hand crept toward his crotch. The speedometer inched upward.

You really don't want to try that ever again, he'd say. *You know you love being Daddy's special girl.*

* * *

Valerie hardly slept a wink all night. She kept turning her pillow, trying to find a patch to put her cheek against that wasn't hot or damp with tears or both. She might have known they wouldn't let her live with Aunt Marge. She would have to tell for it to make any sense. Then it would be her word against her dad's. He'd be the convincing one, because he was a grownup. Or he'd make good on his threats. Even if he didn't kill anyone, even if she was believed, they might not let her live with Aunt Marge. He said if anyone found out, they'd send her to a foster home or some kind of awful group home or detention center for troubled kids. It had the ring of truth to it. She'd heard of families where child welfare got involved and they took the kid out of the home instead of the grownup who was bothering the kid.

So she had to go back. And she'd vowed it wouldn't happen anymore. That left only two choices: kill her dad or kill herself. She didn't want to die—never taste hot cocoa again or see how the shadows turned blue when you looked out the window and saw snow falling through the dark on Christmas Eve. She didn't want to leave Stevie all alone in that house either. She didn't want to make Aunt Marge cry. Anyhow, if she killed herself, Dad won. So she had no choice. Dad had to go.

If nobody believed she was being molested, they wouldn't believe she was a murderer either. They wouldn't think had a motive. She'd seen enough Miss Marple on TV to know that all she needed was means and opportunity. And her mom mustn't be suspected. That meant she couldn't use Mom's pills to poison him. Maybe she'd trip him on the stairs—tie a rope across them and call him from the bottom. If all else failed, she could pretend to go along with it one more time, then stab him when she had him at his most vulnerable. She'd always been so docile that he certainly wouldn't expect it. Could she plunge a knife into his flesh? She wasn't sure.

"Valerie! Are you awake?" Aunt Marge peered around the bedroom door. "Merry Christmas! Hot cocoa and Christmas cake in twenty minutes, and then presents and blueberry pancakes for breakfast!"

Valerie decided that she might as well enjoy every moment of sweet freedom before she had to go back. She drank two mugs of cocoa with marshmallows and whipped cream and ate a piece of cake. Then she put away four blueberry pancakes with butter, powdered sugar, and maple syrup and five strips of bacon, along with a bowl of sliced fresh strawberries and more whipped cream. Aunt Marge had wrapped her presents beautifully. She was good at that, as well as at coming up with gifts that Valerie would love. Valerie was undoing a wide red satin bow very slowly when the doorbell rang. Aunt Marge went to the door.

"Sandy! I didn't expect you so early. Merry Christmas! Come in and have some cocoa. You must be frozen. Valerie, it's your mom."

Cooing and fluttering, Aunt Marge whisked Valerie's mom across the room, unbuttoning her coat and peeling it off her, brushing snow off it, settling her in a big chair, and wrapping her fingers around a mug of cocoa. She finally stopped fussing long enough to notice that Valerie's mother wasn't acting very Christmassy.

"Sandy, is something wrong?"

Mom had a way of starting a story at the very beginning.

"Chet thought it would be better if he came and picked Valerie up yesterday evening," she said.

She couldn't tell it any other way. If you tried to rush her, she simply went back and started over. So you had to be patient while she picked out a path through the details.

"There was black ice on the highway," she said, "and a drunk driver in a pickup truck ran right into him. The poor man was killed outright. His wife was waiting for him at home. She didn't know he'd been drinking. They were going to make eggnog. She said he'd just gone to the mall to pick up a last-minute present for her. The police officer told me she kept saying, 'It was something he knew I really wanted!'"

Aunt Marge couldn't stand it anymore.

"Sandy, is Chet okay?"

"Valerie, honey, I'm so sorry," Mom said. "Your father is dead."

"Valerie," Aunt Marge said, "why are you laughing?"

* * *

It was the best Christmas Frances had ever had.

* * *

Years later, as they decorated the tree with Solstice symbols, Valerie told her partner, "It was the best Christmas I ever had."

* * *

Elizabeth Zelvin is the editor of this anthology. Her stories have appeared in *Ellery Queen's Mystery Magazine, Alfred Hitchcock's Mystery Magazine, Black Cat Mystery Magazine,* and

Mystery Weekly, along with a variety of e-zines and anthologies. They have been nominated three times each for the Derringer and Agatha awards for Best Short Story and been listed in Otto Penzler's *Best American Mystery Stories 2014.* She previously served as editor for the 2017 anthology *Where Crime Never Sleeps: Murder New York Style 4.* Liz's series are the Bruce Kohler Mysteries, featuring a recovering alcoholic and his friends in present-day New York, and the Mendoza Family Saga, which includes historical adventure novels and mystery short stories about a Jewish family in the time of the Sephardic Diaspora, Columbus's voyages, and the golden age of the Ottoman Empire. Liz is also a psychotherapist and addiction professional who has worked with the homeless and developed and directed a women's alcohol treatment program. She has done clinical treatment online for many years with survivors of abuse and trauma. Her author website is www.elizabethzelvin.com.

Pentecost

by Eve Fisher

I t was a big deal when Darla Koenig was inducted as the first female pastor in Laskin, South Dakota. Small towns are highly resistant to change, and even though it was 1990, there were still many people in Laskin who didn't believe women should be pastors at all. Luckily, none of them were members at St. Paul's Lutheran. But then, as Jack Elstad, the pastor of First United Church, said, "Country churches have to take what they can get these days." His wife, Joan, capped it: "After that scandal with the church secretary and the organist? St. Paul's is lucky to get anyone."

Darla was a widow with one daughter, Berry, in grade school. They moved into the Dakota View Apartments, a cheap rental on the first floor. Portia Davison, one of Darla's parishioners, reported after a welcoming get-together that the Koenigs had a lot of old furniture and more books than anyone would know what to do with. Janet Olson, the school librarian, said Berry was smart as a whip. Wade Sillerson said Darla looked a lot older than he remembered, and he didn't like her hair. Just about everyone tried to get her on one of the committees, clubs, and boards in town, but she told everyone that she had to get established before she could tell where she could do the most good. Linus Scholte, pastor of the Netherland Reformed Church, said, "Where *she* could do the most good? Maybe the idea is to do *her* good by letting her in and showing her how we do things around here." His wife Joanne said, "Maybe she's shy," without looking up from her knitting.

Berry was wild about dancing, so Darla signed her up for ballet classes. They met on the third floor of the old Laskin City Building, in a large space with genuine hardwood floors. Laskin was an old-fashioned town, and almost every little girl still took piano or ballet or both for at least a year or two. Since boys also took piano lessons, there were half a dozen piano teachers in town, but Mary Lenvik was the only dance teacher. Her monopoly—and her marriage to Orville Lenvik, the VP of the local bank—meant that she had the leverage to persuade the city to let her put up mirrors along one wall and portable barres despite the fact that the room was also used for various meetings.

"Wow!" Darla said, looking around the dance studio. "This is so huge compared to the old armory. That's where we used to take dance classes."

Mary Lenvik cocked her head slightly. "When was that?"

"Almost forty years ago. I was six years old and chubby with it. Mrs. Bodegaard was the teacher, and she did not hesitate to let me know I had no future." Mary's foot lightly tapped the floor. "But I loved it anyway. I'd have done more, but my father got a job down in Lincoln when I was nine, so we moved, and my ballet career ended. It's a shame you don't have showers up here. I remember how sweaty we all used to get." Mary winced. "But this is great. I'm renting the space at the end of the hall. Our apartment's too small to work from home, and almost everyone at St. Paul's lives in Laskin, so this will be handier for office hours."

* * *

Darla settled in. Her daughter was happy at school; she was reasonably happy at St. Paul's. On ballet nights, she worked late, and sometimes she went over to watch her daughter and the other girls practice. The sound of their feet slapping, sliding, thudding on the sprung wood; the familiar smell of young sweat; the multiplication of curved arms in the mirrors; the sound of classical greatest hits—all mingled in a hypnotic nostalgia that sometimes hurt.

Everyone seemed amazed how quickly she learned everyone's name and found her way around, forgetting the fact that she'd actually spent her childhood there. Sometimes Darla found it hard to believe herself. Joan Elstad, Mrs. Bodegaard's daughter, had been the star of the ballet classes and obviously well on her way to a big city ballet company. But there wasn't a scrap of that left in the expensively dressed woman who drank far too much at every social occasion. Darla remembered her parishioner Portia as a heavyset, plain teenager whose eyes were always sad or shifty. Never married, Portia had ballooned in weight, but her eyes hadn't changed. Wade Sillerson had been so bright, so quick, and a senior prom car wreck had made him lucky to be able to work bagging groceries at the supermarket.

And there were all the people who had come after she left, like Mary Lenvik, always dressed in a leotard with skirt or pants, her blonde hair in a tight bun, a choker around her neck. Back in Darla's time, everyone would have laughed at a grown woman dressing like a child, but not anymore. Instead, she had somehow become the leader of Laskin society, and it would take years to find out how or why.

That was the kind of thing that distracted Darla as she tried to study or write sermons. One late afternoon she was stuck, absolutely stuck, so she went to sit in the dance studio for a while. Portia Davison slipped in ahead of her. It surprised Darla when she saw Portia go into the dressing room and especially when she heard an unmistakable ripping noise. Curiosity aroused, she went into the dressing room, where she saw Portia putting tape on a window.

"Windows? In the dressing room?" Darla exclaimed.

"Used to be the Mayor's office was in there," Portia said, "and this was his secretary's office." She smoothed the tape and stepped away. "Guess they figured a secretary didn't need that much room to work in, and besides, good idea to keep an eye on the help. And the studio was where the City Commission met. Then Pat Corvill became mayor and he wasn't going to walk up all these steps, not with his arthritis. So they moved it all downstairs. And when they rented out the place to Mary for the dance classes, this area was the only place to put a dressing room, so we painted over the windows." She stood up, her face flushed. "They need a touch-up every once in a while. I'll actually paint them over later. Sometime when he's not in."

"Oh," Darla said. "Well, that's nice of you to keep up with it."

"I'm the janitor. Not the caretaker, just the janitor. Can I ask you something?"

"Of course."

"You know that sermon you did for Pentecost? 'And when

He comes, He will prove the world wrong about sin and righteousness and judgment.' And you talked about how every tongue of flame that was there then would come again and burn up every wrong?"

"Yes." Darla could see the suffering in Portia's face.

"Do you believe that? How?"

"Because..." Darla swallowed hard. "That's how I'm still breathing."

"I heard your husband died."

"Yes. He had a massive heart attack. Out of the blue. Even though he was thin as a rail and jogged every day. We'd just had Berry. Our miracle child. I was almost forty, and we never thought we could. She doesn't remember him at all."

"That's hard."

"Yes. But at least Jim got to see her, enjoy her for a couple of months before he died. There are people who have been through worse. That's one thing I've learned in the ministry. People have always gone through worse."

"It doesn't make it any easier," Portia said.

It wasn't until a couple of nights later that it occurred to Darla, sitting up with a hot flash at three a.m., to wonder whose office was on the other side of those windows. Why would they need touching up? Did the girls pick at them? Why would they do that? Not that girls don't do crazy things. They picked the scabs off their knees and elbows same as the boys. They did crazy stuff like jumping off the top of the Kesslers' eight foot fence, built to keep the Kesslers' dogs inside, straight onto hard concrete. Mona broke her ankle, and they kept doing it just the same. Or the time, back in the last year of grade school, on PTA night, while everyone was in the auditorium, a bunch of them had snuck into the boys' restroom to see what it really

21

looked like. She chuckled. And of course, there was Binnie Benson, so desperate to get a boyfriend she had actually let that awful Kevin Watson—

Wait a minute. Portia had put the tape on the inside, where the girls were. But the paint was being chipped off on the office side. Whose office was that, anyway?

The next day she walked down the hallway, past the City Engineer's office, the women's restroom, the elevator, the dance studio, to the office door marked *R. F. Olson, Attorney-at-Law*.

She'd only seen the back of R.F. Olson on the stairs and in the hallway. She'd smelled him, the reek of cigarettes detailing his comings and goings. Even standing outside his office, she could smell the nicotine—his window must be wide open—seeping through the cracks. It disgusted her.

She knocked on the door, but he wasn't there. Back in her office, she tried to work on her sermon, but had no luck. Her mind kept trying to figure out why she was relieved R.F. Olson hadn't been there.

The knock on the door startled her. Emmie Norred, at eighty-five one of the eldest of her St. Paul's flock, peered in.

"I hope I'm not interrupting. Now I'm only going to stay for a moment. I have to meet the Red Hatters at Mellette's at two, and I can't miss that, can I? Now the first thing is that I just want you to know how much we are all enjoying having you as our pastor. I was one of the ones who pushed for you. I thought it was high time we had a woman pastor in Laskin. Too many men for too long. Always on about wifely obedience and submission, which is mighty handy if you just want to have your own way. And worse. Well, there's a lot of wickedness in a small town, as Miss Marple would say."

22

She winked, and Darla nearly laughed out loud.

"I love Miss Marple, a lot more than that know-it-all Poirot. But anyway, I was asked to ask you if you'd mind if the Ladies' Bible Study met in the church again."

"Again?"

"Yes. We used to, but then Pastor Dokken—oh, he was always on about old-fashioned virtues and Pauline doctrine. He wouldn't let us meet in the church. Said it wasn't fitting, unless a man led it. Women could only meet in houses." Emmie's china blue eyes snapped with anger. "Now, granted, the food was wonderful, especially at Rose Skein's who's the best baker of us all, but it's the principle of the thing, don't you think? I always felt that our Bible Study was just as valid as the Men's Bible Study, and they had that every Wednesday morning. Right in the sanctuary! What do you think?"

"I think you're welcome to hold your Bible Study whenever and wherever you like," Darla replied.

"Wonderful. Thank you so much. We appreciate it, we really do. The worst of it was, of course, that it was that Don Olson who led the Men's Bible Study. You know what he did?"

Darla had heard all about Don Olson, organist of St. Paul's, and his flaming affair with Susan Dokken, the church secretary. Both of them married to other people. In Susan's case, to the head pastor. Susan had embezzled money for the two to run away on and was doing six years in prison. Don had left town.

"Exactly. And there he was telling us all what we women should and shouldn't do. Thank goodness those days are over now." Emmie gathered her purse and got up to go. "You're doing a wonderful job."

"Thank you."

As she saw Emmie out the door, a man passed them and

went into his office: R. F. Olson.

"Roger Olson," Emmie hissed. "Don's uncle."

"Roger Olson," Darla repeated. "Was his father Orville Olson? They used to live on South Fourth?"

"That's the family. Orville died a few years ago. Before the scandal, thank God. Well, thank you again, dear." She patted Darla's arm and added, "You come and join us some time for Bible Study."

Darla sat down heavily in her chair. Roger Olson. Olson was such a common name in South Dakota that it had never occurred to her that this was the Roger from her childhood. His parents and hers had played bridge together. They'd alternate houses. She'd go with them to the Olsons' house and Roger would be there. Her heart was pounding fast now, and the heat flooded up her throat to her face.

The parents in the Olson kitchen, playing cards. She and Roger, sitting in the den, watching TV. A western. And he grabbed her hand and put it on his pants. He rubbed her hand up and down the hard fly. "Do you know what that is?" he asked. She shook her head. She hadn't known at all. He got up, shut the door, and when he turned around, his pants were at his ankles, and there it was. Somehow she had managed to run past him, to where the grownups were playing cards.

"What is it, honey?" her mother had asked. "You look like you've seen a ghost."

Her mother, concerned and alert; her father, waiting to see if he needed to be. Mr. Olson, looking only at his cards. Mrs. Olson, looking at her with an expression she hadn't understood then, but that had scared her. Now, thinking back, Darla thought she had looked defiant.

Child Darla knew she didn't dare say anything. No one

24

would believe her. And even if they did, something about the incident—and she hadn't been sure what it was or why—but something about it even happening to her would taint her. She shouldn't *know* that something had happened. She shouldn't *know* that it was bad.

So she'd just said, "I don't feel well. I think I'm gonna be sick. Could we go home?"

Her mother reached out a hand and felt her head and said yes.

And that was that.

And she'd forgotten it, she would have sworn that she had forgotten it until now. Well, not entirely. She'd told her husband about it. Once. She'd said it was long ago and it didn't matter. Just showed how sick some people were.

Though it might have had something to do with her going into the ministry.

But she would have sworn that she wouldn't have thought about it ever again, if Emmie hadn't told her his name, confirmed his address. And now that man had an office behind those windows where her daughter, where an endless stream of daughters, including *her daughter*, would dress and undress. In front of that line of windows

Darla found Portia in the first floor lavatories, cleaning.

"Portia," Darla said, "how long have you been checking the windows in the dance studio dressing room?"

Portia's eyes shifted, as if she was looking for a way out. "Theresa Heilman came down here all upset one night. Said someone was looking through the window in the dressing room. So I went up, and sure enough, he'd scraped a hole in the paint."

"He being?"

Portia rinsed off her broad red hands and dried them. "Roger Olson."

"Were you surprised?"

"Not really. My oldest sister, she warned me about him. She said back in school, he was Mr. Touchy-Feely, Peeky-Parker. But always by accident, you know? So he never could get caught? He hasn't changed much." There was bitter resignation in her voice. "Most people don't."

"Why don't we just paint over the windows on the girls' side of the dressing room?"

"Because. Mary Lenvik's allergic to the smell of paint. She doesn't want the girls to be alarmed. She doesn't want them to talk to their parents. She doesn't want them to talk among themselves. And she's sure that Mr. Olson would never do that." Portia took a deep breath, and Darla felt her whole upper body burst into flames. "She won't even agree to put curtains in there. Someone might ask why. The town might be embarrassed."

"This is insane!" Darla burst out. "This has got to stop. Now."

"How?"

Darla tried to think what they could do, and the long silence that followed was extremely nonproductive. There was no proof. There was no "harm" done. He hadn't touched any of the girls. He "just" liked to look.

Finally, Darla said, "This has been going on a long time. Roger wasn't right when I lived here." Darla felt her heart hammering. "He exposed himself to me in his parents' house. While they were playing bridge with my parents. I was eight years old. For God's sake, what did he think he was going to do?" The cry burst out of her. "That was almost forty years ago. And I'm sure I wasn't the first. Or the last. Who knows who else he's exposed himself to?"

"Me," Portia said to the floor.

"Oh, my God," Darla said. "I'm so sorry." She put her arms around Portia. "Of course. I should have known. I'm so, so sorry—"

"How could you have known?" Portia interrupted, pulling away from Darla. "Do I look like a victim?"

"No," Darla said. "Because you recognized a victim when you saw one."

Portia burst into tears and let Darla hold her as she wept.

"It's all right," Darla said. "We'll do something. We'll think of something. We can report him. We can—"

"Pastor Koenig," Portia said. "Darla. I don't know many women in this town who'd be willing to admit that something like that happened to them. And we don't have any proof. He's a lawyer. His dad was mayor. He hangs out with Judge Dunn and everyone on the City Commission. To them, Davisons like me are trailer trash, and you're not from around here, not anymore. Nobody's going to listen. And people might get hurt. Especially the girls."

Portia was right. To speak up would mean that every ballet student for the last twenty years, but especially the ones right now, would be pointed out, whispered about, objects of pity but also of suspicion, sullied just because someone had seen them, might have seen them, naked. Everyone would discredit Portia just because she was a Davison. To speak up and be doubted would ruin Darla's image, if not her reputation. Darla would be called a troublemaker and a feminazi and every other misogynistic slur, and it would be another ten years at least before there would be another woman pastor in Laskin.

And it wouldn't even matter whether they were believed or

not. Even if they were, Darla and Portia would be hated for opening the can of worms, and the girls would still be held somehow at fault.

It wasn't fair, it wasn't fair, it wasn't fair.

"I've got to think about this," Darla said, and went for a long, long walk.

That night, during the dance class, Darla got up and walked past Olson's office. There was a dim light behind the shade. After the class, Darla sat in the car with Berry, chatting idly, making up excuses not to drive away, until she saw Roger Olson come out the door and head home himself.

The next morning, Darla went over to the dressing room. A new peephole had been scraped on Roger's side.

* * *

The Laskin Fire Department received the call at 10:05 p.m. Friday night: a fire on the third floor of the old Laskin City Building. When they got there, they found Pastor Koenig standing outside waiting for them.

"Oh, please hurry!" Darla cried. "I think it's the dance studio. Or maybe next door."

By then flame was licking its way out of one of Roger Olson's office windows. The fire department managed to contain and then put out the fire. The third floor reeked of smoke and wet ashes, water was everywhere, Olson's office was heavily damaged, all the floors were filthy from the firemen's boots, but otherwise, the city had gotten off lightly. The rest of the building was fine.

The insurance investigator and the fire department agreed that Olson's smoking—which was illegal in the city-owned building—had caused the fire, but it was accidental, not arson. The rumor about hard liquor and pornographic magazines was never proved but spread widely. Even so, Roger couldn't rent another office in any city building nor from his fellow attorneys. No one wanted another fire.

It took two months to complete the repairs and remodeling—the interior windows had broken in the fire, and it was made into a solid wall—and provided everyone with plenty of entertainment. Portia became Darla's shadow, and a lot of cups of tea and coffee were shared in Darla's office, which hadn't been damaged. Mary Lenvik joined them sometimes. Over time, Mary decided that Roger's old office would be perfect for a central Laskin Arts Office for herself and other arts leaders in town and talked the city commission into it. The Dakota Singers, the Arts Council, and the dance classes would split the rent, and everyone felt pretty sure that Mary would make sure their contributions would cover the dance studio as well.

Darla stayed on in her office. That fall she started a Women's Christian Book Club that met there on Wednesday nights. When the ladies arrived that first September evening, they found written on a whiteboard:

"Why indeed must 'God' be a noun? Why not a verb—the most active and dynamic of all?" — Mary Daly, *Beyond God the Father: Toward A Philosophy of Women's Liberation*

"What does that mean?" Portia asked.

"It means God's not male, right?" Emmie Norred offered.

"Exactly," Darla replied. "Another Pentecost. And this time, we're all included."

* * *

Eve Fisher's mystery stories have appeared regularly in *Alfred Hitchcock's Mystery Magazine* as well as other publications from *Tough Crime* to *Black Cat Mystery Magazine*. Her work is currently being translated into Chinese by a fan in Shanghai. A retired university history professor, Eve still writes historical articles (primarily on patterns in history), including "The $3,500 Shirt—A Lesson in Economics," which appeared on the BBC and became part of an economics textbook. She also writes science fiction, and "Embraced," in the *Startling Sci-Fi* anthology, was nominated for a Pushcart Prize. Eve is the president of the Alternatives to Violence Project in South Dakota, which puts on monthly weekend-long workshops on non-violence for inmates in South Dakota prisons. She lives in South Dakota with her husband and five thousand books. Her website is www.evefishermysteries.com; she's part of the mystery writers' blog SleuthSayers.

The Call is Yours

by Rona Bell

I n New York City, we all dress for the street. We dress for
strangers in a way we never dress for friends. The street
led me to you. Now, so many years later, I can't see you.
But I am calling out to you. I am shouting into the crowd in
my mind, and I am making a single telephone call.

I have spent a lifetime perched in an office tower, first behind
a typewriter and then a computer and now a sleek laptop, and
if I live long enough I will just type in the air. For all these years
I have looked down at the street, down to the corner of 57th
Street and Fifth Avenue, the very heart of desire. This is the
stage of New York, where women who want to twirl and show
their finery gravitate and turn in circles and hope that men will
glance with shining eyes. The entire crowd here has eyes like
fireworks. Not the orchestrated fireworks over the East River.
No, the quick flashes of light from the firecrackers parents give
to children, who run through the dark night on the wet grass
of the Midwest before growing up and setting out for the big
city. I thought of the fireworks so many times, looking down

to the corner of 57th and Fifth and watching desire come to life. There was a special man there. And you were there too, over the days, over the nights, and I am speaking to you as though you are here before me.

You and I both watched that special man. His name was Bill Cunningham. Now dead, he was the fashion photographer for the *The New York Times*. I thought of him as my guard. Whenever I looked down on the street he was there with his camera, scanning the street, waiting for the perfect emblem of the fashion of the streets. He was a hatmaker before he was a photographer, and I watched him, always drawn to the hats, scanning the women who were new beauty itself.

I wanted him to photograph me.

I did. I plotted it, I thought about it, and I knew the heart of the secret, that Bill Cunningham would never photograph anyone who asked for it. If a woman stood on the corner and posed, she was making it too easy. Look at the lace around my knee. Look at the hair pins with birds on the end, studding my hair somewhere between hair pin and hat. Bill Cunningham, prowling through the crowd like a low moving panther, with his camera lens moving out in front, a predator looking for the next meal.

I whispered about this with another woman in my office. Laura.

Do you remember her? And if you do, do you remember her name? Every day she wore a different hat, the hats the English call fascinators. The men in the office never looked at her with sparks in their eyes. But I knew her hats were custom made. *Bespoke.* That was the word she said to herself each day as she sat down. She was the woman I wanted to be. I know you admired her hat.

Laura always sat at her computer as though she was in the moment just before the model walked out on the runway. She would wink across the room to me. I would nod my head and lift my chin to acknowledge her hat. Sometimes I would give her a thumbs up to say good luck as she set out exactly at noon.

I knew where she was headed each day. Laura would push herself back from her typewriter like a ballerina pushing herself away from the barre. She would brush past me, a hand brushing my shoulder, and then she was gone.

You should know that I watched her from my window.

I knew that Bill was waiting for her in the crowd, and one day she would attract him like some rare bird who floated by with brilliant plumage and with no words, no whistles, attract his lens.

Even more I loved to watch him, how he loved women, how he stalked them in the jungle of New York, dancing through all the women who wanted to bask in the click of his camera that echoed all through the city. Laura and I talked about this. She told me that it was never good form to twirl in the middle of the sidewalk. She said if you caught the photographer's eye there was no chance that he would ever take your picture.

I believed that I learned everything about how a man approaches a woman from her, from her talking about wanting the flash in front of her eyes, how she wanted to be known to be beautiful and then to savor a moment when the workday was done. The whole point was to wait through the work week and all the grinding noise of the city and the push for completion of work that did not matter.

But recognition mattered, and it unfolded in the Sunday paper. I saw it in front of me one time. I was on line for New York bagels, that essential component of a weekend. A woman

33

seated in the corner opened the *The New York Times* as though she was opening a giant fan of peacock feathers.

"Oh," she said, "here I am. I am in Bill Cunningham's column." She paused and said, "Again."

The entire line in the bagel place and the men smearing cream cheese on salty bagels and the women squeezing lemon on their Nova, they all stopped. The people in line heaved a collective sigh. The woman had done it. The newspaper fan closed and it was done.

Laura was out there that noon. There was no sun that day. It was the perfect lunchtime for photography. New York seemed, from my window, to be the kind of city you see in photographs of the 1930s. There is no sun, but there is stark contrast, and everything is ready to be observed.

This was the New York that drew us.

And it was the New York that drew you.

I remember that moment, and I can open a gash in my memory to remember every second.

Laura waited for the light to change and then, like a deer emerging from the woods, she walked across the road and let all the cars, all the yellow cabs watch her, wait for her.

And then she was there, in a pool of light and on the corner of 57th and Fifth. She was all alone. New York City can be like that. Everything parts, and a person can be alone for a time, only for a moment. There can be solitude in the middle of a crowd. That is one stunning thing about New York City.

I saw Laura reach up to check her hat and the waves of black hair settling all around the hat and lifting her up. She wasn't looking for anyone.

And in the moment, as she lifted up her arms and a black handbag dangled at her elbow, there was the camera.

Bill Cunningham appeared as though from a cloud. And his camera pointed up, the long lens right up to her red hat. There was the click. And then another. Laura turned a half step, drawn by the click of the camera. She did not try to catch Bill Cunningham's eye. He was crouched beside her, down by her side, and then sprang up. If he were an escaped animal, he could have ripped her head in a single bite and been gone.

But this was the art of the center of fashion. I saw Laura continue walking, her back straighter, Bill Cunningham looking into his camera lens and checking the shot.

I expected her to come back to the office and wink at me. I wanted to hear the story, wanted us to leave our typewriters and head to a coffee shop where she would tell me everything about what it was like to be photographed by Bill Cunningham. I would learn from her.

I watched her and imagined her quick step back to me to strengthen the deep ropes of meaning that built up the friendship between women.

But instead, you appeared.

You were right behind Bill Cunningham. Just after he took the picture, you stepped out from behind his shadow as though you were dancing. Your leather shoes shone despite the gray day. You put your arm around Laura's waist. She jumped but then relaxed. You shook her hand. I saw you talking, leaning low down to her and nodding. You could have been the mMayor, bestowing the greatest honor known to New York.

Laura walked with you, a block and then two and then out of my line of sight.

Laura came back to the office an hour later, slinking at the edges of the wall, and sat down. She avoided my eyes. Her head

35

sank low. Her fingers reached for her keyboard, her perfect nail polish sparkling but her eyes down. She no longer had her hat.

Maybe it was not wonderful to be photographed. Maybe she did not share with me because I would never understand. I was not the girl who could giggle and share. Maybe she would do that with someone else.

We did not speak again.

But every day at noon Laura went out to the same corner. I watched her. She was not photographed again.

I saw you wave to her, nod to her, slide up behind her. She tucked her head down and touched her hat, the blue one now, and turned away from you.

Two weeks later she did not come to work. When I looked down into her typewriter I saw the long metal fingers like a skeleton hand. Dead, without someone moving the keys, dead. There was no explanation. Around the office, people only shrugged. Someone else took her place, and the keys danced.

It was a different time. Women hunched over typewriters could vanish without leaving a forwarding address when they headed out to another coast, another man, another job. She could have had a secret baby. We accepted all of that and none of it.

But after Laura left, and I don't know why, but this chains my heart and my thoughts, I wanted to try my luck. I wanted to be photographed. Laura never made it into the actual newspaper. It might have been better if she had. But maybe I could unfurl myself and set off into the block of 57th and Fifth and make a twirl.

There was no one in my life.

Now that I was chained to a computer rather than a typewriter, I believed I had lost my soul.

I could be immortalized, or I could be dead. Either would be fine.

Now I see that was a terrible thing. It was maybe what drove the salmon upstream, fighting, when a bear could lift them up into the jaws of death, or they could make the next generation.

Does a woman like me want to circle the possibility of being taken by force? I turned that thought around in my mind for days, and it played like water circling the drain while I chose what I would wear when I headed to the street, dressed for New York City and maybe for you.

Here is what I selected, in case you do not remember. I wore a dress with a splash of color on the left sleeve, something brave and filled with circles of yellow and orange with a gash of purple in the middle. The rest of the dress was nothing more than a sheath, the thing we wore then. From one angle, I would be invisible. From another, I would be wild. I was wearing everything inside me on the outside of one sleeve.

I tucked a black bag in the crook of my left arm and left my desk. A man smiled at me in the elevator.

"You are going for the walk," he said.

I smiled. He knew. I was going into the ring to try to be photographed, to try and attract the one man, the one photographer, who could seal my beauty.

And that is how it was with me.

The sun was a spotlight right above the corner of 57th and Fifth. I walked to the end of the block, as though it was an accident that I was there. I was on my way to a meeting, to a man, to a new job. To something new, anything new.

And there he was, swiveling at the end of the block. Bill Cunningham's camera scanned the edges of the crowd. A woman behind me yelped. Bill, with his animal hearing, moved two steps away. He would not take her picture. And in that moment I passed before him. He leaned down toward me, camera first, the long lens snaking out toward me. But he was focused on the white side of my elbow. There was nothing there. That was not the right side. No. I turned so that he could see the pattern, the slashes and the wide poppy shapes that covered a single side of my arm.

But I had turned. I had shown myself, and in that moment I had begged him to capture me, to take my picture. I knew it as I did it. It was a twirl that created an invisible rope between us, a rope with spikes that I believed would turn him toward me. But Bill had made a career of knowing when women wanted it, and when their need for an approving gaze showed itself, his camera went dark. In that moment, Bill turned away from me, and his camera lens pointed down at a man with a glowing leather briefcase and a dog collar around his puppy that matched the briefcase exactly.

I was walking in the wilderness. There would be nothing for me. I turned back to my office tower, the tower that cast a shadow over me, and it was done.

In that moment I thought I should leave New York. I came here and no one admired me. I was silent and hopeful and wanted something I could not name.

There was a woman I saw once. She did not have a job, not like me. Her hair was askew and her purse was battered, but I saw her at noontime leaning against a Tiffany window and wanting something in there or someone to see her. Did she not know that the diamonds in the window were fake? They were there for tourists and for people who slid into the store and bought the real thing. But she did not belong there, and as she leaned on the glass, her eyes half closed, maybe drunk, maybe just wishing, a security guard appeared behind her, and in a moment he placed his hand on her waist and moved her, with reverence, away from the window. In that moment she thought he had chosen her to dance, and she lifted her arms, framed by the sparkling glass diamonds behind her, and then, when it was clear there would be nothing, her arms fluttered to her sides and she drifted away.

If I was not careful, that would be me. That is what I said to myself, and then I saw you.

I saw your shiny brown shoes, the color of a caramel cat, and felt your warm hand splayed across my back, supporting me and then digging into my ribs.

I felt safe.

How could that be? But I leaned against you, and you guided me.

"You are beautiful."

You said that, and I smelled the sharp odor of sweat, but then it mingled with my Chanel perfume and the smell of the dust of Fifth Avenue that sprayed up from the crushed rocks.

"Don't worry," you told me. "He will take your picture another time. You have to be ready. I will make you ready."

Any other woman, I think that any other woman would have moved away at that moment. That was the moment to steer myself back into the crowd and away from you.

But I did not. I did not do that. Instead I took a step toward you, and for one bright New York street-lamp second, I wanted to believe that you were right. You could get me ready, whatever that meant.

We were dancing in the streets of New York, where you guided me by my back. In that next second, I imagined you guiding me into an old dark bar on a side street and ordering a drink that could be drunk at noon, and you would tell me of your life, how you shadowed Bill Cunningham, how you were there in this special role that could only exist in a crowd.

When I look back, it is remarkable to me how much can take place in a moment, how much can take place in a minute and then shape the course of an entire life.

You guided me, or I followed. You possessed me with no more than the touch of your hand, right there. And then I followed you step by step. I was wearing those shoes with the red soles, the ones that women whispered were a sign that men always understood. We whispered those words and we all wore the shoes.

And then we were in a crack between two New York buildings. I was only steps from my office. I knew that, I had passed this alley, swept clean because this was the best address in New York.

You lifted my dress, your fingers touched me. I leapt with the fire of it, the surprise, the welcome and the dismay.

And then you were done.

You did not guide me back. You left me there, gasping in the dry air of the alley. You walked away and I saw you nod, as though you were counting.

When I looked up, there was one strip of New York sky, one black cloud moving fast over my head.

And then when I looked to my right, there was a single gash of red on the wall.

Lipstick, I thought, lipstick from the woman who was here before me. But no. My finger hovered over the slash. Blood.

And with that I slipped out of the alley and into the sunshine and looked to the heavens to ask that the light erase that moment and everything that I did to draw that moment toward me.

I read the *The New York Times* every day, and every Sunday, I looked for the women that Bill Cunningham had captured. More than once I saw you in the background, eyes alight. Those days, I think there were three of them, I spent Sunday in my bed, under the covers, hiding from the light.

How our bright city draws women toward it, asking us to do the one great twirl of our lives. Either we climb to the top of the Empire State Building or we fall into the gutter that floods with every rain.

I wonder what happened to the woman who leaned against the Tiffany window. She may have become a model strutting the streets of New York. From time to time I think I see her. I wish her well.

Laura never came back, no one ever heard from her. I never said a word to anyone about her. I never saw you on the street.

But twenty years later, the New York Police Department ran an ad campaign it called "The Call is Yours," encouraging women to come forward. They said no crime was too far in the past to be investigated. Then I did another kind of twirl. I called. I told them first that I believed I drew you to me, that I pushed myself out onto the street, trying to be something that I was not. I told the detective that I am better as a watcher. I have watched for years. I have kept my soul to myself. But I told the detective about Laura and the one red gash that must still be in the alley if graffiti hadn't overtaken it or a building had not collapsed and been reborn.

The detective asked if I would take her there.

I said *Yes*, in the clearest voice I could manage. We met at the corner of 57th and Fifth, and I walked her to the alley. I showed her everything, including that one red mark. It was faint, but it was still there. When I went to trace it with my finger, she grabbed my hand, and I felt the charge of healing, a panther's paw with a camera on her arm.

"The call was yours," she told me. "You have done enough."

* * *

Rona Bell is the pen name of a well-known New York business executive. She has published (under other pen names) in the *North American Review*, the Akashic Books *Mondays are Murder* series, as well as such publications as *The The New York Times, The Washington Post,* and *Business Insider*. Her most recent piece, "Spies on the Street," appeared in the Summer 2018 edition of *Mystery Readers International.* Her short story, "Prey of New York," was included in the anthology *Where Crime Never Sleeps: Murder New York Style 4* and listed in Otto Penzler's *Best American Mystery Stories 2018.* Rona is a graduate of the University of Rochester, received a graduate degree from the University of Michigan, and is proud to have studied with Jonathan Santlofer at the Crime Fiction Academy. She has always been interested in the concept of opposites and the possibilities for story between those two extremes.

The Final Recall

by Diana Catt

I sat alone in the darkened microscope room watching for error messages to appear on the computer screen and adjusting the robotic back-and-forth movements of the modified transmission electron microscope. Five years of post-graduate research landed me this hyped-up fellowship where I used all the same skills as the cashier watching the self-checkout machines at my grocery store—but with less pay and no benefits. The big draw in this position was the chance to work at this university's world-class neuroscience research center with Nobel laureates Dr. Roger Kolb and Dr. Stephen Yeager. Quitting before I had at least one publication would be professional suicide, and I was not yet suicidal.

The door behind me opened, sending a shaft of light across my screen. I pulled out my earbuds and turned as Dr. Arvin Turnstone, one of my collaborators and fellow post-doc, entered.

"There you are, Sara. How's everything going in the dungeon?"

"Same as usual. Dark and mysterious. What's up?"

"Kolb wants to move the progress committee meeting to seven a.m. on Friday. Okay by you?"

"Yep."

"Great. Come out for air every so often so you don't go stir crazy."

"Too late, man. I'm already there."

"Right. See you Friday, then." He closed me back into the gloom of the electromagnetically shielded room.

I repositioned my earbuds and reached over to flip a switch, turning on a salt lamp I'd positioned in the far corner. Maybe I'd hang up a crystal tomorrow. Working on cadaver sections didn't bother me, but having good energy around couldn't hurt. The computer screen flashed an error message, and I made the appropriate tweak. Images emerged, starting as fractured partial scenes, then eventually expanding to become a single three-dimensional video of someone's stored memory. The software I was testing assembled data from sequential brain sections. The computer shuffled signals and read interconnected synapses to pull together memories from the convoluted storage processes of the brain. Then it digitalized those molecules to form a computer re-creation of an individual's memory. It could take days or weeks to fill in all the details of each separate memory image. A very dull process for the person monitoring the controls. Namely me.

The big picture of our research project was cool, though. We brought memories from dead people back to life. It was a blind study, so I didn't know who the donor had been or whether or not they suffered from some form of dementia. Each cadaver was identified by a code indicating the gender and age at death, but any other identification could bias our interpretation of the results. What we'd interpret was a cohesive memory in the form of a video. We'd already had success with static pictures, and we were still working on translating nerve impulses to audio.

One cutting-edge breakthrough at a time.

The images, all from the cadaver's point of view, were striking and showed remarkable detail. The computer read and translated the molecules and pulled components together based on parameters such as location details, facial character-istics, hairstyle, clothing colors, and activities. However, we had no way to verify whether any of the memories generated by this software were real, false memories, or artifacts of a computer glitch. After nine months of gathering data, I feared I could be putting my career on the line for cutting-edge, computer-generated crap.

Three hours after Arvin's visit, I was still in my zombie stupor, closing in on the last of the brain sections from Cadaver F23-109, a twenty-three-year-old female. With only twelve more slides to read, the computer was rapid-fire hopping around between multiple nearly complete memory scenes as the microscope passed across neurological strands sending molecular information to be decoded by our test software. For a nanosecond, a disturbing scene appeared on the computer screen. By the time my mere human brain registered something interesting, the computer had skipped through multiple additional images. I stopped the program and reversed the data until I found the image that had caught my attention.

I yanked out my earbuds and sat up straight, hardly believing what I saw.

I had that same memory! No kidding, I remembered that

scene. It was the break room here at the research center. I recognized Carla, the technician from Dr. Yeager's lab, who organized numerous social gatherings that I always tried to avoid; Pierre, a cute post-doc fellow in Dr. Yeager's lab, who charmed all the women; Abigail, a technician from Dr. Kolb's lab and one of my closest friends; and Doreen, the department administrator and keeper of all knowledge. There were some other people I didn't have names for, but I knew their faces. Smoke poured from the microwave—I remembered that happening. I knew the fire alarm was blaring and the odor was horrible. And there, that was me, hurrying across the room. Holy shit! I'd been in this subject's memory.

As my own synapses fired, I realized several important points. I shared a memory with this cadaver. She had been here at the research center shortly after I began working here. And I would have a very interesting proof-of-function reveal for the progress committee meeting on Friday. *I* was proof that this was a real memory, not a composite thrown together and filled in by the computer software. There was hope for my career after all.

My elation collapsed as an additional implication seeped in. Those paper-thin brain tissue sections in the tray belonged to someone I might have known. Whatever barrier I'd been using to distance myself from the humanity of all those brain sections cracked wide open. I wanted to cry for this woman, this almost friend, this almost me.

Who the hell was she? I racked my brain to remember who else had been in the break room the day of the microwave fire. This center had lots of visiting scientists and temporary work-study students coming and going, making it almost impossible to know everyone, even if I wasn't isolated in this room most of the day.

I was sure I'd have heard if someone in our community had died. But the proof was right in front of me. Someone who had been in that break room with me was now dead, her brain partitioned onto these research slides. She must have felt strong ties with this facility to donate her remains for research. Ethically, I shouldn't have done it. But I couldn't resist taking a closer look at her results.

I zoomed in on every detail of the fire alarm memory. I noted what I wore, what the others in the image wore, how Pierre smiled and beckoned to her as he exited the break room. Then her gaze returned to me as Dr. Kolb grabbed my arm.

"Other way," I remembered Kolb yelling at me over the scream of the alarm.

Dr. Yeager was right behind him, shouting for everyone to hurry.

"My purse!" I said. "It'll only take a sec."

"No exceptions," he said. "Follow the herd outside."

I watched myself turn toward the exit. Smoke poured into the scene and I couldn't see anything else.

I hit Pause.

I remembered what happened to me next. I found my friends huddled under a tree away from the smoke as the fire trucks pulled up to the building.

"If my notes burn up, my life is ruined," Abigail was saying as she paced in little circles.

"If the power goes out, my cultures will die," Pierre said. "Three weeks wasted! I head home in five weeks. I have to be done by then! What am I expected to do?"

"Don't worry," Carla said. "It was just the microwave. I saw it. We'll be back inside within twenty minutes, I'll bet."

"Thank heavens for that," I said. "The microwave burned up?"

"No, something inside it," Carla said. "I saw flames. Who doesn't know how to use a microwave?"

No one ever owned up to overcooking the bag of popcorn. A new microwave was brought in the next day, but the odor of burnt popcorn and charred paper hung around the break room for longer than anyone expected.

Odors. Another memory component our technique had not yet captured.

All the faces in that memory were familiar. If I asked enough questions, I might figure out the identity of F23-109. And break all the confidentiality regulations on the books. Too late now, though. Obsession had already overcome ethics.

I knew who to ask first. The department administrator would have a record of everyone who was working at the research center on the day of that fire alarm. I stopped my program, hit Save, locked up the microscope room behind me, and headed to Doreen's office.

The administrator's door was open, and I gave it a quick courtesy knock. I couldn't ask Doreen who in our department had died and donated their body to research. That would invalidate all my data and result in so many complications I didn't even want to think about it. Ironically, my shared memory could either be used to validate the whole system or just as easily to invalidate it. I needed to proceed with extreme caution. So I just asked for the date of the popcorn fire. She was annoyed at the interruption but supplied the information.

In my rush to get back to my computer, I backed out, nearly colliding with my boss, Dr. Kolb, as he stepped through the open door.

"Is there a problem, *Dr.* McGuire?" he asked in that dismissive tone, fixing me with his characteristic scowl.

"No, sir."

"Well, then, back to the grind."

"Right," I said. What an ass. It wasn't just me, though. All women got that implied challenge to their degree from him. I always wavered between wanting to prove myself and wanting to kick him where it hurts.

The rest of the day I obsessed over Cadaver F23-109's memories. I returned over and over to her file, searching the data bank of her captured lifetime of memories, trying to zero in on anything related to our research center—colleagues she worked closely with or socialized with—that could provide some clue to her identity. This program was all about piecing together related fragments to form a complete memory picture. So I could ask it to match the people from the fire alarm memory with their images elsewhere, if any of them appeared elsewhere in this subject's memories. I saved those images to a separate file.

I started with myself. I drew a box around my face in the fire alarm memory and ran a search of the database. Nothing popped up. Did our paths only cross on this one occasion, or was there a glitch in the system?

Maybe she just didn't look my way on any other occasion. Since she liked Pierre, he was a good candidate for a search. In fact, he turned up in several other images—smiling, laughing, listening, gazing into her eyes. Usually they were here at the research center, but occasionally at a restaurant or someone's home. Unfortunately for me, Pierre was gone, so I couldn't quiz him about the subject's identity. Again, I saved these memory images to my special file.

Other people from the popcorn memory, as I now thought of it, were still at this facility—Carla, Abigail, and Dr. Yeager. I searched for Carla's face next. Up popped additional memories in which Carla appeared. In one, a short video of images, Carla was sitting at a table, eating, talking, drinking beer. In the background was an old red brick wall hung with pictures of the Blues Brothers. I recognized the city's oldest bar, a favorite lunch destination for research center staff. These memories also went into the special file.

I ran equivalent searches with Abigail and Dr. Yeager but came up blank. At the end of the day, Cadaver F23-109 remained unidentified.

Before I left for home, I ventured down to the morgue. Judy, the tech who prepared the tissue sample slides for my research, would know how old the samples from Cadaver F23-109 were. None of our subjects were supposed to be dead for over a year.

"Can you check your records?" I asked.

"Sure," Judy said. "Let's see. Her death date meets the requirement."

"Hmm. Well, I'm seeing anomalies, lots of partials, like we see when there's degradation. Not like with dementia, though. It's behaving more like some of the sample sections are missing. Is there anything in the notes?"

"Says she died of trauma to the cranial region. But that doesn't seem to have affected the areas you've requested. We had the right number of sections."

"Well, something is sure wrong about this cadaver. Can you check the death date again?"

"Last August 4. Puts her well within the specs."

"Okay, it must be something on our end. Sorry to have bothered you."

"Doesn't bother me. But I just found a note in this case file. Apparently, someone should've called the boss before releasing samples from this one. Shit's gonna hit the fan."

I didn't see why it would bother Judy's boss. But it bothered me. She had died the day of the popcorn fire. Our shared memory was one of her last.

The next morning, I found Carla enjoying donuts in the break room. I picked out a Bismarck, poured myself a cup of coffee, and joined her at the table.

"Who brought in the goodies?" I asked.

"Yeager," Carla said.

"Hey, do you remember the microwave fire about six months or so ago?" I asked.

She nodded. "Yeah. What brings that up?"

"Nothing, really, I just ran across it in my notes. Brought the whole thing back. That nasty smell. And, I remember how worried Pierre was about his experiment."

"Yeah, he was in full panic mode that day," Carla said, "but it turned out all right. He finished up on time."

"And that friend of yours you hung out with a lot back then?"

"Who's that?" Carla asked.

"I can't remember her name, but she liked Pierre, I think."

"Oh, you mean Monique. Yeah, she had a thing for Pierre, and they spoke the same language. Ooh la la." Carla's eyebrows arched up a few times.

"Both from France?"

"Well, no." Carla reached for another donut. "Pierre was, but Monique was from Montreal. She left about that time. Pierre seemed annoyed that she didn't tell him goodbye. She didn't tell me goodbye, either. I guess we weren't that close after all. She didn't even leave a forwarding address with anyone."

Monique was not in Canada. She'd been dead in the morgue all this time. Pierre and Carla didn't have a clue.

"No, wait," Carla added. "Pierre thought she might have taken that position at Adelaide University in Australia she was considering. She used to joke about running to the opposite side of the world to get away from him. Why are you asking?"

I wondered if she'd been in an accident on her way to the airport. She must have left in a hurry, then dropped off everyone's radar.

"Seems a little weird," I said.

"Well, you know how people come and go around here. I can tell you that she and Pierre had a big fight. He was jealous about someone else. You might ask your Dr. Kolb about her, if you're really interested," she added.

"Kolb? Why? She didn't work in my lab."

"No. She worked in Yeager's. Pierre accused her of having a thing for Kolb," Carla said. "Yuck."

"Uh-oh, TMI," I lied. "I am *not* going to ask him about her, that's for sure."

So now I knew my subject was named Monique. Monique might have been involved with my boss, Dr. Kolb. And now Dr. Kolb's own team was investigating Monique's memories. Did he realize she was dead? Should I tell him? It would take an ethical wizard to figure out the right way to handle this. My stomach turned. I tossed my half-eaten donut in the trash.

I had the means at my disposal to verify a relationship between Monique and Dr. Kolb, but I didn't relish the idea of making that search. I didn't want to think about it, let alone see it. I had tremendous respect for Dr. Kolb's work, but the man himself continued to disappoint.

I unlocked and entered my domain. The overhead light was

on, and I never left the light on. My first thought was to blame Housekeeping. Then I noticed my workbench. The boxes of slides were in disarray. Housekeeping would never mess with my samples. Not only was it unprofessional, but they knew the risk of touching biohazard materials. I reorganized the mess, then realized several boxes of slides, including F23-109, were missing. Holy crap! Who would steal my samples? My data! Did they sabotage that, too? Dread overwhelmed me. I turned on my computer and tried to pull up my data files. Nothing. Nine months of research wiped off my computer in a locked room. I dashed to the hook on the wall where my lab coat hung and checked the pocket. I found my flash drive right where I left it. Thank goodness! It was a good thing I always backed up my files at the end of the day. My life wasn't in total ruin.

I headed straight to the post-doc office I shared with Arvin, where I could get a phone signal.

"Arvin, you're not going to believe this. Someone deleted my data and stole some samples."

"What the hell?" he asked. "How did that happen? Didn't you lock up?"

"*Of course*, I locked up! I always lock up. I always turn off the light, too, but it was on when I got there. Several sets of samples are missing, and my data files are gone."

"Did everything get deleted?"

"Hang on a minute. Let me call Security."

Arvin became increasingly agitated as he listened to my end of the call. As soon as I disconnected, he pounded me with questions.

"Did you lose everything? Why didn't you have a backup? This is a disaster, Sara! Years of our work destroyed!"

"Annoying, yes. Disaster, no. Take a breath, Arvin. Everything was wiped from the hard drive, but I have it all backed up. And I'd finished the analysis of the sets of samples that are missing, so it won't slow things down too much."

"What a relief. But who would do this?"

"I have no idea," I said. "I was hoping you'd have a clue."

Arvin shook his head. "Lots of people have a key to that room. Just in case, maybe you'd better keep the back-up files locked away in the vault back in the storage room."

"What vault?"

"Come on, I'll show you before Security gets here."

I followed him down to the end of the hall. He unlocked a door and I trailed after him into the room. He locked it behind us.

"Let me have the flash drive," he said.

I pulled it out of my lab coat pocket but didn't turn it over.

"Where's the vault?" I asked, looking around the rows of file cabinets.

He pointed to a small fireproof box in the corner.

"That's it?" I asked. "And I suppose whoever has a key to the microscope lab can also get in here. I think I'll make a couple more copies first, if you don't mind. I've got a lot of time invested in this project."

"Suit yourself. The key to the safe is in this front cabinet."

"Seriously, Arvin? You call this security? Never mind. I bet Doreen has something better in her office."

"Whatever. You need to tell Dr. Kolb about this, you know. He's going to blow a gasket."

"You have the memory program on your computer, don't you?" I asked.

"Sure."

"Can I use it real quick to make more copies of my data," I asked, "before I call Kolb?"

"That might be a smart move," he said. "I believe in active self-preservation."

I copied the data to Arvin's computer. The simultaneous arrival of two Campus Security officers and Dr. Kolb prevented me from making a copy to a second flash drive as I intended. I spent the next hour recounting the discovery, protecting my remaining samples from getting hauled off to forensics, and facing an angry boss. Throughout the ordeal, I kept one hand in my lab coat pocket, fingers securely wrapped around my flash drive.

The police took a list of the missing samples—F23-109, M23-010, M28-011—and I explained the numbers meant they were a twenty-three-year old female, a twenty-three-year-old male, and a twenty-eight-year-old male.

"Is there anything special about any of the people these samples came from?" the woman officer asked.

I couldn't tell anyone about my popcorn memory until I told the progress committee.

"Not that I'm aware of," I said. "This is a blind study, so we don't know who they are. I suppose Judy in the morgue could tell you more if you need it."

"That's ridiculous," Dr. Kolb barked. "It will take permission from the lawyers at an Internal Review Board to release any information on these subjects, unless you get a warrant. They weren't the target of this vandalism anyway. They're all dead! You imbeciles need to find out who wants to sabotage our research."

Dr. Kolb bared his teeth and roared about the exorbitant cost of this research and how the whole project might be indefinitely delayed without suitable replacement samples, and he would hold the whole Security department and these officers personally responsible. I tried to assure him that I had all the data backed up, but I couldn't tell if he heard. Kolb continued to berate the officers, me, Arvin, housekeeping staff, and even the building's lack of a security camera system. Meanwhile, I found the boxes of missing slides smashed and broken in the break room trash can. After that, the Security team didn't seem too concerned. The officers wrapped up their questioning and left.

By the time I got the microscope room back in order, salvaging all the broken bits of microscope slides from the trash, it was almost the end of the day. I grabbed a coffee from the break room and repeated the story of the theft for about the millionth time as people passed through on their way home. I looked forward to getting in a couple hours of uninterrupted work before heading home myself.

I hadn't made a conscious decision to search Monique's memory file for images of Kolb, but when I finally opened the program and reloaded all my data files, it seemed like the thing to do. I felt a kind of sisterhood with Monique, hoping to prove she wouldn't have been involved with such a volatile man as Kolb. Those who say a researcher should not know too much about the subjects under study are right.

I pulled up a picture of Dr. Kolb from our research center website and ran the search. To my dismay, Monique had encountered Dr. Kolb often. Without examining the memory images, I saved them into my special file for F23-109. I saved all my data onto another flash drive, just in case one backup wasn't enough. Then I examined the results of the Kolb search.

My boss stared back at me, or at Monique actually, with a

lecherous smile on his face. Thankfully, I'd never been on the receiving end of that look from him. Monique succumbed to that combination—powerful guy and sex—because that was the point of most of her memories of him. It was as nauseating as I feared. I hated my task, hated myself, but I kept looking. The last memory I opened was the same smoke-filled break room of the popcorn memory, and Kolb came into view. He led the way out of the room, but not toward the exit. Instead, Monique followed my boss down a deserted hallway into a file room—the same file room with the ridiculous safety "vault" that Arvin had shown me earlier today. Kolb's expression changed from aroused to angry, and his fist shot forward. Memory over.

Was life over for Monique at that moment also? I hated being a voyeur. I wanted to cry. I wished I could go back in time to when all my subjects were simply tools of the trade, not real people who might have a death memory.

I opened my email, attached a copy of this last memory, and typed in Arvin's, Carla's, and Doreen's addresses. I typed *Monique's Final Recall* into the subject line.

The door to the microscope room opened slowly. I looked up and met that chilling, angry expression from the memory I had just witnessed.

"You should have come to me," Dr. Kolb said. "We could have avoided this."

"Sir?"

"You went to Doreen. You went to Judy. Who else have you spoken with?"

He had seen me in Doreen's office. Judy from the morgue had said there was a note in the case file to call the boss before releasing F23-109. But she meant my boss, not hers. Kolb had found out I'd been asking questions about Monique.

He must have been shocked to learn that Monique's brain sections had been included in his own research study on memory.

"You didn't know she was in the study, did you?" I said.

He closed the door behind him.

Karma exerts itself in strange ways. That last memory of Monique's—one more proof that this damn technique worked. Was my last memory also going to be shared with Monique?

The only light in the tiny space came from my computer screen, which was open to my email page. Kolb couldn't see my trembling fingers on the keyboard. As he approached, I hit Send. I swiveled the computer around to show him the image.

"You hid her body in the morgue as a donation subject, didn't you? I found her final recall."

Kolb's curse reverberated through the enclosed space. He glared at me, then reached down and yanked the computer cord out of the wall, plunging the room into complete darkness. As he wrapped the cord tightly around my neck, I tried to twist away, smacking at his arms without effect. I couldn't breathe. I fought to relieve the excruciating pressure on my windpipe. I couldn't even wedge a fingertip under the cord.

He yanked and jerked my body upward out of the chair. I was going to pass out. Oh, God, I was going to die. I reached out into the darkness toward my desktop for anything to use as a weapon against him—a pen, my keyboard, my thermos. My hand scrambled across the surface until I felt the broken slides. I latched onto one and sliced behind me, connecting with my attacker's arm. His grip loosened a bit, and I managed a ragged breath.

"Bitch," he said in a venomous tone and re-tightened the

cord.

I lashed out again, aiming for the source of that hate-filled voice. This time he let go of the cord completely, and I scrambled away.I fell across my overturned chair as I ran through the dark toward the door. I tried to yell for help, but I could only produce a raspy noise. I stumbled into the postdoc office. Arvin gasped and caught me before I collapsed.

"Oh, my God, Sara. You're bleeding." He examined my hand.

"Not me," I thumbed toward the microscopy room, took a big breath, and wiped my bloody hand on my lab coat. "It's Kolb. Come on. It's bad."

Arvin turned on the overhead light and gasped. Kolb lay across the floor in a pool of blood. I detected refraction in the slashed tissue as I bent down to check for a pulse. The jagged glass had severed his carotid artery. In true karmic symmetry, the label on the shatteredslide read F23-109.

* * *

Diana Catt has fifteen short stories in multiple genres appearing in anthologies published by Blue River Press, Red Coyote Press, Pill Hill Press, Wolfmont Press, The Four Horseman Press and Speed City Press, as well as a collection, *Below the Line*. She is co-editor of *The Fine Art of Murder* and *Homicide for the Holidays*. Her short story "Framed" appeared in The Best by Women in Horror anthology, *Killing It Softly 2*. She is co-author of a play, *Deadbeat,* which debuted at the 2018 IndyFringe. Diana has three grown children, two grandchildren (ask to see pictures!) and a doctorate in Microbiology. She teaches microbiology at a central Indiana university, owns an environmental testing lab, and likes hunting in scary places for mold. Find more at www.dianacatt.com.

A Measured Death

by Julia Pomeroy

Mary looked at her watch. Ten after five. Late, late, late. Jan would be so angry. Two blocks away, she could see the maroon awning of her building, but her short stride seemed to be making little progress on the long pavement.

She was carrying two heavy bags of groceries, so she couldn't wrap her arms around her body for extra warmth. Instead, she leaned into the wind that was ripping down Central Park West and tried to walk faster. Maybe she should have used some of her allowance for a taxi, but she hated to waste it on transportation, and cabs in New York felt like money thrown away.

When she finally walked up to the lobby, Manuel, the day man, appeared at the heavy glass door and swung it open, welcoming her into the warm.

"Hola, Mrs. Raz. Why you walkin' again? It's cold out there. Here, let me take those bags." After ushering her in, he moved ahead of her to the elevator and pushed the call button. The door slid open. He held it while she got on.

Mary liked Manuel. When she was alone, he always had something nice to say, a joke, a thoughtful gesture. Sometimes she even thought he was flirting with her. But she wasn't sure, she'd lost all sense of that over the years. He was probably just paying her a little attention because he felt sorry for her. Luckily, when she passed through the lobby with Jan, he was much more formal. She was grateful for that. Friendly would only get her into trouble.

As the elevator traveled up to the penthouse floor, Mary glanced at herself in the beveled mirror. She saw a small, gray-haired woman, her nose red from the cold, her shoulders beginning to stoop. She thought briefly, with a flash of irritation, that she looked like an old, scared rabbit. Ridiculous to think that anyone would flirt with her.

The elevator came to a halt on the eleventh floor, and the door slid open. Manuel carried the bags and put them outside her door while Mary dug inside her purse for her keys. She could hear Jan inside the apartment. Before he got back in the elevator, Manuel winked and put his index finger to his lips. Mustn't disturb the great man.

There was one other apartment on their floor, and Jan had tried a number of times to get Mrs. Goldman evicted. He wanted to turn her one bedroom into a music studio, but she had lived there forever and was now the last rental tenant in the building. Her apartment was rent controlled, and as long as she lived there, observed the rules, and paid what she owed, there was nothing the co-op board could do.

Mary put the key into the lock. They had two pianos in the apartment, but Mary recognized Jan's beloved Bösendorfer Imperial Grand. Wherever he performed, he always insisted the concert hall bring in a Bösendorfer, even when he didn't need the extra octave. He said the sound was more resonant, more nuanced than that of a Steinway, and anyway, after all these years, it was his trademark. He was right, of course. The classical music world expected its great artists to be idiosyncratic and demanding, even difficult. And the classical music world adored Jan.

Mary listened. He was having trouble getting the Rachmaninoff concerto back into his fingers, so he was going after it relentlessly, brutally, practicing six or seven hours a day, as he always did before a concert. Mary knew that the pressure would build and, eventually, he would conquer it. By the time he walked out onto that stage he would be ready, the program flawless. Yes, he was truly a master.

The thought gave her no joy.

* * *

Mary often looked back in wonder to the time when she'd met Jan. Those faraway days at Juilliard seemed to be populated by a different species, and she had trouble reconciling them to the couple she and Jan were now.

In those days, Jan Razinsky was one of the darlings of the Professional Program, a brilliant young Polish refugee who, while performing with a Russian orchestra on a supervised visit to London, had managed to escape his Soviet watchers and make it to the American Embassy. He even looked like a pianist: thin, his Adam's apple sharp on his long neck, waving dark hair swept off his high forehead, a strong beaked nose. His hands were large, his fingers veined and still.

She, Mary Ferri, was his opposite. Small, blonde, with a

round chin and deep dimples, Mary wanted eventually to teach music after her performing career had peaked. She was a first-year undergrad from Muncie, Indiana, had never been away from home, and knew no one in New York. He was twenty-five, she was eighteen.

The first time he noticed her was outside the practice rooms. They were both waiting for pianos, listening to the muffled sound of a student struggling through Chopin's Winter Wind étude. Jan caught her eye and shook his head.

"It does not always make perfect, no?"

Mary blushed and grinned, happy to be included in the joke, even though she wondered what he would think of her playing.

What was it about him that she had fallen in love with? It was more than his dramatic look that reminded her of portraits of Chopin or his rich, chocolaty accent, his obsessive talent. It wasn't just his elitism which, once he included her in his favored circle, elevated her above the crowd.

It was the romance of his escape from tyranny, the passion she imagined he felt at the fulfillment of his lifelong dream to reach the West. In her most private moments she admitted that she saw herself as the incarnation of the West, like the sensuous and draped Liberty, welcoming the young renegade artist.

In bed, she had responded to his over-muscled fingers and hands, his pianist's bulging forearms, "like Popeye's," she thought, feeling goofy, knowing that Jan would neither understand nor like the reference. He told her, lying next to her, his voice serious and low, that he loved her and needed her. Within a month she gave up her apartment on West 94th Street and moved her few possessions into his cramped fourth-floor walk-up nine blocks from Lincoln Center. One of Jan's wealthy music-loving patrons gave him a baby grand. They had all they needed. She was gloriously happy.

Six months later, when he had visa problems, the solution was obvious to Mary. She suggested they get married.

He kissed her hand and said, "Yes, but not just for immigration business. We do it to be like Musketeers, no? Two for one?"

Mary laughed happily at his mistake. She had never felt so loved.

The marriage was easily done. She had no family in the area, just her aging father in Indiana. They tied the knot at City Hall, the only guests three other pianists that Jan knew from his program. At the time, her only friends were two Juilliard dancers, Peter and Vincent, neighbors in her old building. She didn't invite them because Jan confessed they made him uncomfortable. He didn't explain. She thought that maybe, because of his upbringing, he wasn't yet comfortable around homosexuals.

On their wedding night, she lay in the dark, wishing that her mother had lived to see her marry such an amazing man. Wondering what her mother would have said to her that day.

* * *

Within a year of their marriage, Jan had won first place in a major piano competition. He told everyone that his delicate little American bride brought him luck; that he could concentrate completely on his work, knowing she was by his side. The prize was a contract with the most prestigious management firm in New York. From there it would be a small step to bookings, tours, and eventually, his first recording.

Ten months after winning the prize, Jan asked her if she'd look after his scheduling; he was so busy it was hard for him to stay on top of it.

"And you, my darling," he said, standing behind her, cupping her breasts, his long fingers easily overlapping each other across her small torso, "you don't want me to hire a beautiful secretary, do you?"

She smiled happily. "I'd kill you."

"Of course you would. So you will be my secretary and come on tour with me to Europe."

Mary's laugh died. He must have forgotten.

"I can't go, Jan, I have school," she said, taken aback that he would ask, twisting around to look at him.

"Why do you want to go to school? I am making money and will soon make more, just for you."

"But I have to finish, you know that. I want to teach."

That's when he said, "Please, Mary, my love, you cannot teach. You have no talent, why would people want to learn from you? No, you must come with me to Europe."

She was stunned. She backed away from him as if he had slapped her.

When he saw her reaction, he said softly, taking her chin in his fingers, "I'm sorry. I do not mean to hurt you. But we must be honest, no? You would tell me, yes, if I was not talented?" And then, playfully, he waggled her chin up and down, as if she were nodding in agreement.

He continued in his still choppy English that until then she had found so delightful, "I love you, so I tell you. You are not good musician. You are very short, so your hands are small. Look at you, you cannot span one octave! You are a beautiful sexy woman. But not a great musician. I need you.

Without you, I cannot be great. Good, yes. But not great. Please. Students don't need you, I need you. Musketeers, no?" And then, when she still didn't answer, he added, "Maybe next year we begin our family, you would like that?"

Years later, she wondered if that had been her one chance. If she'd told him to forget it, take a hike, bud—ridiculous idea, he wouldn't have known what she was talking about—that she was going to teach, talent or no talent, that she was going to finish school, lousy musician or not, she might've had a different life. But she didn't. Because he was right, of course. His was the great talent. As a lover of music, she could see that. And how could she argue with the truth, however much it hurt?

She didn't speak to him for an entire day. He bought her flowers and grapes, as if she were an invalid. A week later she took a leave of absence from school and started packing for Europe.

One year later, over dinner, she told Jan she was ready to go off the pill and have a baby.

He frowned and told her, no, not yet, there was no time. He couldn't have a baby in the house.

"My career is at last showing success. I need your attention, your love. I cannot hear a baby crying near me."

Next year, he added, when things settled down.

The next day, more flowers, more grapes.

And so the years went by. Jan's career grew and solidified. Soon he was performing all over the world to sold-out houses. Eventually, his recordings came to be considered part of the library of American masterworks. And Mary looked after his home and his comfort, answered the phone, and shielded him from unwanted attention. He became her life. She had no friends of her own—they were all Jan's people—musicians, critics, composers, wealthy society ladies and their bill-paying husbands who liked to consider themselves patrons of famous artists. She was close to no one.

After they'd been married some fifteen years, Jan began to worry about his health. His father had died in his fifties of a heart attack, and Jan was afraid he would do the same. He went to a series of doctors, sure he had some inherited heart defect. They did a variety of tests and assured him his heart was strong. He would feel better if he exercised. He shrugged off their advice. Instead, he insisted that Mary take a course in CPR, in case he needed emergency help.

"There is no one else who can look after me like my little wife," he said to her.

So Mary took a class at a downtown hospital. When it was over, Jan insisted she go to every concert he gave in case he needed assistance. She was to sit in the green room during the performance and listen to it over the intercom. And she was to stay there when the performance was over and his fans lined up, single file, to meet him and pay homage.

Mary did as she was told. She sat there and knitted. She had no one to knit for, but she made scarves and little babies' hats and booties and gave them away to the Salvation Army. She wondered if people whispered about her, because she rarely spoke or smiled, but she didn't particularly care.

Over the years Jan took on a few students, mostly female, all attractive. Some he kept, others he discarded, telling them they should give up the piano and take up cleaning houses, because that's all they were good for. And if he discovered one of his male students was gay, he would dismiss him, saying that only a real man could play Beethoven or Brahms. Not a half-woman.

He stopped wanting her for normal sex. In hindsight, she wondered if things had started to change soon after the last time she said she wanted a baby. Maybe he thought she would trick him into getting her pregnant, go off the pill without telling him, so he decided to use only those orifices that wouldn't do the trick. She came to dread his loveless and brutal grindings, and her only relief seemed to be when he had a pretty young student who became the temporary focus of his attention.

When these students came over, Jan would tell Mary to go out, disappear, until the lesson was done. She would go to the movies or, if the weather was good enough, sit in the park. Sometimes she walked across to Fifth Avenue and went into FAO Schwarz, through the relentlessly cheerful sound of the song that came out of the giant clock. "Tick tock, tick tock, welcome to our world of toys," it sang with metronome-like precision, the chant of young voices enveloping her, hypnotizing her, pulling her in.

She would wander through the store, humming the song, wondering if any of the awestruck tourists were from Indiana, watching the nannies and their charges, the mothers and their sweet, happy children.

When it came to money, Jan was always generous. That is, he controlled it all, but he gave her a large weekly allowance for food, clothes, and household expenses. So they lived well, ate well, dressed well. He insisted on that—she was his wife, after all, and he expected her to look elegant. Their apartment was large and showy, with a beautiful view of the park.

Mary, however, wasn't a co-signer on any of the accounts and knew nothing about Jan's finances. When her father died,

Jan had insisted that whatever the old man owned be sold to pay for his funeral. The small house in Muncie that she had grown up in was in poor repair so she sold it for forty-three thousand dollars, paid eight thousand to the funeral home, and Jan took the rest, telling her he would invest it for her.

* * *

One Saturday, just before her forty-ninth birthday, Mary was walking down Columbus Avenue, thinking about a pair of shoes she wanted to buy. She loved shoes and often spent whatever was left over of her household allowance on a new pair.

But that particular afternoon, she heard someone calling her name, her maiden name. "Mary Ferri!"

She looked across West 73rd Street and saw a tall, heavyset man smiling and waving to her. His sparse hair was dyed an improbable carroty red. It took her a long moment to recognize Vincent, her old neighbor from West 94th Street. She would have dodged him, but for all his size, he moved quickly. He crossed with a bounce to his step and took her in a big bear hug.

Once she got over her surprise, she was happy to see him. Gone was the beautiful dancer with the toned, sleek body. In his place was a man past middle age, run to fat, face jowled and sagging. They went to a coffee shop and caught up.

She found out that poor Peter had died of AIDS in '89, and Vincent had given up dancing a few years later. He had moved to California for close to ten years and come back when his mother had taken a turn for the worse. He now worked part time at the Drama Book Shop and painted *trompe l'oeil* murals on commission. He was married to a man he had met a year earlier online.

"We did it in Vermont, in case they changed their minds," he said. "But enough about me! I've followed your husband's career." He flashed his eyes at her. Vincent might have left the stage, but he was still full of performance. "He's done so well, but I've looked for some mention of you, our little Mary Fairy, on the Internet or whatever, but nothing! Not a peep! I was sure you'd be concertizing like mad, with your connections. What happened? Did you just decide to quit? You were so good!"

When Vincent finally hurried off, Mary stood on the corner outside the coffee shop, staring after him. When she finally stirred and looked around, she felt as if she'd just woken up from a trance.

Three blocks south, Mary went into a bank she knew Jan had never used. When she was finally seated across from an officer, she put what was left of that week's allowance on the desk in front of him.

"I need to open a savings account."

Over the following months, her shopping habits changed. She began to look out for bargains and sales. She bought cheaper cuts of meat, darned her clothes, even had her favorite shoes resoled. She cut coupons from the newspaper. And at the end of every week, she put whatever was left of her allowance into her new savings account.

For the first time in years, she had a purpose.

By the end of the first year, she'd saved $4,027.24. By the same time a year later, $10,145.03. She did all her banking in person and insisted that no paperwork be sent to her house. The account was her dark, frightening secret. Whenever she thought about it, she flushed with heat, as if over a lover.

* * *

One January evening she was about to go into her apartment when she heard the lock turn in Mrs. Goldman's door.

The old lady was now in her nineties, her fingers bent with arthritis, her lips eternally red with high-gloss lipstick. Mary liked her, but her affection was colored by guilt because of the attempted eviction. Mrs. Goldman seemed to have no idea that her neighbors were behind the push to get her out. In fact, she claimed to be a lover of piano music and delighted in saying to him, in her raspy voice, "I'm the lucky one, dah-ling, I don't pay Lincoln Center prices to hear the great Jan Razinsky. I can hear him for nothing, all while I'm sitting on my toilet! Who else can claim that, I'd like to know?"

Jan would nod and smile when she said it, but when he turned away his face would pull into a sneer of disdain, his full lips curling up to his nose. *"Kurwa,"* he would spit out in Polish, once they were inside their own apartment.

Mrs. Goldman was wearing a robe and slippers.

"Mary, I'm so glad it's you." She sounded terrible—congested and hoarse. Her eyes and nostrils were ringed in red, her lips for once pale and bloodless. "I have a rotten cold, dear. Do you have a thermometer? I had my old glass one, but I dropped it, old butterfingers me."

"Of course, Iris. I'll be right back."

Mary slipped inside the apartment. She could hear Jan at his piano, his fingers hitting the keys with the strength and evenness of silver hammers.

In Jan's bathroom, she hunted through the medicine chest

72

until she found his digital thermometer. He was always afraid of getting sick before a performance, so he checked his temperature daily, considering it the best indicator of fitness.

Holding it in her hand, she turned to go. Jan was standing in the doorway. She hadn't noticed that the Bösendorfer had fallen silent.

"Oh, Jan." She felt her heart give a loud thump, like a faulty furnace that might possibly break down. "I didn't hear you."

"Why are you going through my things?" he asked, looking at her face, not what was in her hand, as if he already knew what she was up to and was waiting for her to lie.

She waved the thermometer like a small wand.

"Iris Goldman's sick, poor thing, I'm lending her this."
He put his hands in his pockets and rocked up onto his toes and down again.

"You must be joking—that's mine. I won't have in covered in her germs. Put it back. With luck, she'll die."

"Oh, but—"

"I said put it back. Do as you're told. And then come into my office. We have something else to discuss." As he turned to leave, he held up his right hand and snapped his fingers.

Ridiculous gesture, but the thermometer rattled delicately against the jar as Mary put it away, in time with the tremble of her grip. He was angry at her about something. What had she done?

In the room that Jan used as his office, the one that, years before, Mary had hoped to transform into a nursery, she found him sitting at his desk.

"I received a call from a bank today."

Oh, no. There was a sudden roaring in her ears. He'd found it, he'd found her secret account.

"A bank? Why?"

He shook his head. "Mary, Mary. I am not a total fool. I have supported you all these years while you chose to do nothing. I have indulged you, given you everything you wanted. Have you ever gone without? No. Have you had to work? No. But now you steal from me. You're a thief. Nothing more. A thief."

"I'm not," Mary said. Her hands were clasped, and she started to squeeze and knead them, twisting the fingers of one hand with the other till they were white and bloodless.

"Now I see, you are also a liar. What were you going to do, leave me?"

"No, no, Jan. I just wanted to feel—"

"Liar. In the morning we will go to this bank together, and retrieve my money. And then you will pack up and get out."

"Get out? What do you mean? Where will I go?"

"Surely you planned for that. Anyway, it's no longer my business. You have lost my trust."

"Jan, it's nothing, I just wanted a little of my own, a little security, I—"

"Was it worth it?" he asked, a joyless smile playing on his lips.

"Please, Jan," she whispered.

That night, she lay awake for a long time, while Jan slept beside her.

Sometime during the night, a storm moved in, bringing hail and sleet with it. Mary could hear pieces of ice clattering against the windows. She suddenly remembered that she had never gone back to Mrs. Goldman and told her she had no thermometer. She could have said she couldn't find it, it was lost. She lay there in the dark staring into the black.

The next day she and Jan set out after breakfast. They walked cautiously on the ice-painted sidewalks. At the bank, they waited in line, and Jan made her get her exact balance from the teller before filling out the withdrawal slip. She held the cash for only a short time before he pulled off his black leather gloves, took it from her, and slipped it neatly into the inside breast pocket of his overcoat.

"And that's that," he said.

Outside, the sky was leaden. It began to snow again. They were at the corner of 72nd and Columbus when a voice called out: "Maria! I just met a girl called Maria!"

They turned. Vincent was bounding happily toward her.

"We can't go on meeting like this, dear one," he called out, smiling.

"Vincent!" Mary wanted to run to him and throw herself into his arms. She moved toward him, a port in the storm.

Jan, sensing her comfort with the large man, lunged for her. He grabbed her arm.

But on this one day, Mary wouldn't be stopped. She yanked her arm away.

Jan stepped after her onto a patch of ice. Suddenly he was skating, trying to find traction. For a moment it looked comic, then his feet went up in the air and his head back. He hit the cement with a loud thwack.

"Oh, Jesus!" Vincent gasped.

"That was his head!" Mary said.

For a moment, they both stood unmoving, staring down at him. Then Mary knelt beside Jan's inert body and put a hand on his chest.

"Is he breathing?" Vincent said.

"I don't know."

"Oh, my God! I'll call 911," Vincent said.

"I know CPR," she said.

As people stopped, craning to see what had happened, Vincent blocked their view with his large body.

"Please, don't crowd her," he said. "An ambulance is coming. She knows CPR—back away, give her some room so she can help him."

Mary, the building in front of her, her back to the street, adjusted Jan's head. She tilted it back as she'd been taught, so as to open his airways.

She leaned down to put her mouth on his. As her lips approached his, she remembered those long-forgotten kisses, those tender smiles after they'd made love in their first shared apartment, that mouth, full lips curved with pleasure, wide with laughter.

But only for a second. Her hand was resting on his chest, and she could feel the bulge of the cash beneath it. Those delicate memories disappeared like the snowflakes melting on his slack face, and she was left with nothing but the acid years of selfishness and small cruelties.

Her back shielding her movements, the falling snow curtaining her, she held his nose with her right hand and his jaw with her left. She lowered her face to his. Just before their lips touched, she used her left hand to close his jaw, her fingers clamping his lips together.

She touched her mouth lightly on her own fingers, keeping his closed, and exhaled, letting her warm breath slip over her hand and his face. Then she lifted her head, counted slowly to six, and lowered it again.

The people who stopped to watch and those passing were touched by the sight of the woman kneeling in the falling snow, trying to breathe life into her beloved husband.

76

After a few minutes, with the siren getting louder in the distance, she felt his body convulse and struggle. She held strong.

* * *

Today, as she did every day, Mary jogged slowly around the reservoir in Central Park. She was building up endurance. There was an elasticity to her body, a vibrancy to her stride that had been missing for a long time.

When she got home, Manuel, as usual, was there to open the door.

"Hola, Mrs. Raz, lookin' good," he said, cheekier than ever. She smiled at him.

On the eleventh floor, her breathing back to normal, she unclipped her keys from her waist and unlocked her door. She glanced at the door of 11A. Jan had had his way—poor Mrs. Goldman had died from that cold she'd picked up. Actually, it had turned out to be the flu, and she'd gone pretty quickly once she was taken to the hospital. Her apartment was on the market within weeks and had been bought by a nice couple. Mary had already had dinner with them once and was planning to reciprocate soon. She felt that the wife might, with time, turn into a friend. But Mary still missed Mrs. Goldman.

She unlaced her running shoes and kicked them off inside the door. She walked down the hall, her sweaty socks leaving damp footprints on the polished parquet.

"Honey, I'm home," she called out.

Jan's alcove office off the living room was now where he lived, if you could call it that. A complicated mechanical hospital bed had center stage, monitoring equipment and supplies on either side. Dr. Sussman, who had been in charge of his care at NYU Medical, had strongly suggested to Mary that she put him in a special facility for comatose patients. It was, he insisted, Jan's best chance of improving. But Mary said no, he could breathe on his own so she wanted him home, where she could supervise his care and look after him herself. Her love was what would make him better, not a fancy rehab center where no one would care what happened to him.

At the insistence of her lawyer, Mary had had Jan declared incompetent so she could take over his finances. Luckily, he had made dozens of recordings during his illustrious career, which brought in a steady income in royalties. He had also invested wisely over the years, and Mary was happy to continue in the path he had carved for them.

A month before, she had been approached by a publisher and asked if she would like to write a book, with a ghostwriter, about her life with the great Maestro. She hadn't agreed to it yet but had already started making notes and jotting down events that would help her paint a picture of their life together. Other than the flirtations and affairs with students, there was nothing to show that their marriage hadn't been ideal. She had never complained to anyone or run whining to a friend. She had stood by him and encouraged him. Her word was gold; she could rewrite the marriage into the one she had always wanted it to be. She had made poor choices, weak choices in her life, and now was her chance to fix the past.

Not bothering to shower, she went in to see Jan. The day nurse had already come and gone. He lay on the bed, eyes closed. He was pale, his gray hair cropped close to his head, his body flattened under the neat covers. Only his nose jutted out, white and sharp. She had given up wondering if he could hear

78

anything, feel anything, understand. She knew the answer.

"Hello, Jan, darling," she said. "I'm all sweaty—just came back from my run. I wish you could see me. I'm in such good shape these days, you would barely recognize me—I've lost weight, my thighs are strong, my stomach is like a rock. You know," and she sat on the edge of his bed and lowered her voice, "I'm thinking of asking the doorman Manuel to come up here tomorrow." She watched him. "He likes me, and I think I'm going to fuck him. What d'you think?"

She looked for the slightest twitch, the tiniest spasm.

Nothing.

Stepping out of the alcove, she sat down on the bench seat in front of the magnificent ninety-four key Bösendorfer and raised its cover. She didn't need such a fancy piano—if it were up to her, she'd sell it and just keep the smaller Steinway. But the sound of the Bösendorfer was different, and Jan responded to it. She didn't want to give that up.

She wasn't disappointed about his lack of response to her comment about Manuel. He'd heard. He'd just gotten good at hiding it, that's all. And maybe, honestly, he didn't give a crap if she had sex with the doorman.

But this, she thought with a smile, this he cared about.

She took a deep breath and banged both hands down hard on the keyboard. The sensitive instrument exploded into a dissonant crash.

There you go, honey. That should get your attention.

She started her warm-ups, scales that started at middle C and traveled up the keyboard. After all, she was going back to school in a few weeks, and she was rusty after a lifetime away from a piano. But she was improving. When her hands and arms began to tingle, she stopped the scales.

It was time.

Her favorite song, and the only one she really spent any time on. She was going to write a symphony one day, built entirely around this theme.

She began, hitting the keys lightly, humming along as she played the simple tune. Tick tock, tick tock…. She closed her eyes, imagined all the children exploring the store, running from one toy to the next, laughing, squealing. "Welcome to our world, welcome to our world, welcome to our world of toys…" Over to her left she could see Jan, lying on the bed. She watched his face. She saw his cheek twitch to the insidious little tune. His breathing seemed to be getting a little shallower.

She hit the keys harder and increased the tempo.

Though his body was motionless, she imagined his anxiety level soaring—like an underground cavern, bubbling and boiling under the surface.

How he must hate the song. She thought of his heart, weakened, those small genetic flaws growing and spreading, like cracks in fine china. Mary knew that one day, the sound of her at the piano would kill him. But not too soon.

She had so many years to make up for.

* * *

Julia Pomeroy has published three novels in the crime fiction genre, all set in upstate New York. *The Dark End of Town* and *Cold Moon Home* both feature restaurant worker Abby Silvernale; *No Safe Ground* tells the story of a young female Iraqi war vet, her father, and her trans uncle. Though she has written about upstate New York, Julia hasn't always lived there. By some strange coincidence, when she saw the list of contributors to this anthology, she realized that she'd known one of them when she was a child in Mogadishu, Somalia. This is Julia's first short story.

Miss Evelyn Nesbit Presents

by Ana Brazil

"*M*iss *Evelyn Nesbit Presents Her Sweet Revenge!*
What the hell kind of title is that?" H. H. Samson splashed the bottle of champagne toward Evelyn's shallow glass until the bubbles overflowed onto her slender fingers. "The damn picture's got a title already, *Her Eternal Shame.* It's gonna be the most sensational moving picture of 1914."

Not for the first time during their luncheon in the private dining room of New York City's Hotel Astor, Evelyn Nesbit dabbed her damp fingers on the soft linen napkin on her lap.

"I know that you've already got a title, Mr. Samson, but I'm suggesting a new one. And I also have a few suggestions about the storyline. She doesn't have to—"

"I don't allow people to change my stories. I wrote it, and I like it. I'll direct and produce it just the way it is."

But I lived it! Evelyn held her napkin in both hands, twisting it as tightly as she could. The script might have *H. H. Samson Productions* typed on the front cover, but every scene, every title card, every sexual incident in the script was taken directly from her life. At fourteen years old she was befriended and then raped by famous architect Stanford White. Years later she married Pittsburgh millionaire Harry K. Thaw, who shot and killed Stanford. At his trial, where Evelyn was forced to testify about how Stanford ruined her, her husband was found not guilty on the grounds of temporary insanity and sent to a mental institution. It had been over two years since Evelyn and their son had seen him.

For over an hour, Evelyn played the role of H. H. Samson's faithful audience. She sat obediently as he slurped Blue Point oysters, slashed his way through a sirloin steak, and stuffed glazed sweet potatoes into his mouth. All the while, the Asparagus Salad Delmonte that H. H. had ordered for Evelyn turned soggy on the plate. H. H. refused to have the asparagus removed until Evelyn obeyed his command to finish her food. He continued to refill her champagne glass to the rim. And Evelyn continued to empty her champagne covertly onto the Hotel Astor's fine floral carpet.

Although this was a business lunch—to discuss Evelyn's starring role in H. H.'s first feature-length moving picture, five reels and fifty minutes of brutality, depravity, and point-blank murder—conversation so far had been a minimum. Only as the assorted fruit and cheeses made their appearance and H. H. lunged at the interior of a full cream Camembert with his fruit knife did Evelyn make her move.

"I think the world of your script; it's quite a story." Evelyn's eyes brightened as she glanced at H. H. over the top of her champagne glass. They both knew scripts for silent moving pictures contained the bare minimum of instructions. After all, there was no need for dialogue. H. H.'s script was all of five pages of double-spaced typewriting with very large margins. Evelyn's four-year-old son could have written as detailed a script.

"It is a masterpiece," agreed Samson. "A young, beautiful girl, the sole support of her family, toils as a photographer's model. She is pursued by a rich architect who lures her into his fabulous mirror-paneled room where he forces her to ride his plush red velvet swing for hours. And then he rapes her."

Evelyn wanted to slip under the table and hide. Instead, she ran her finger along the stem of her champagne glass; she had not yet discarded the contents on the carpet and suddenly thirsted for a taste.

"Four years later," H. H. continued, "Evelyn—the public's going to love that she's named Evelyn—marries a very excitable, very jealous millionaire. Knowing how his wife was ruined, he plots to avenge her shame. He murders the evil architect in public at Madison Square Garden. His crime leads to the Trial of the Century, and his wife is the star witness for his defense."

Evelyn was sickened at how casually H. H. referred to the most horrific years of her life and how he was using them for entertainment. At both of her husband's trials, Evelyn's sexual past had taken center stage in the courtroom. She'd been forced to detail every brutal perversity Stanford had subjected her to, including the night she could hardly remember—the night he had plied her with champagne, led her into one room dominated by a long red velvet swing and another room paneled with mirrors, and stolen her virginity when she was only fourteen years old. Almost every newspaper in America detailed her testimony: how Stanford had ruined her, how she tearfully explained Stanford's assault to Harry, and how, once she married Harry, he grew increasingly irrational about

Stanford White.

Evelyn anchored the stem of the champagne glass between her fingers and inserted herself into her life's narrative.

"Yes, it's quite a story. After the trial, the husband is sent away to a hospital for the criminally insane. The wife has a baby. The husband's family spurns her and the child. She is forced to seek employment and fails."

Evelyn faltered at the word *fails*. H. H. Samson's picture had finally diverged from her own life. *She* would never fail to support herself and her young son. And *she* would never end her life story as H. H. Samson had ended his picture.

But H. H. Samson demanded the final word on his script.

"The ending—when the wife takes her own life to prevent her innocent son and noble husband from being tainted by the shame of her rape—is the best part of the picture. Everybody says so. You gotta admit, when she kills herself, there won't be a dry eye in the house."

Evelyn swallowed drily and slid her glass just beyond reach, refusing to let a sip of champagne touch her lips. Yet.

"Dessert, sir?" A waiter bent crisply at the waist, offering a large platter of confections for Samson's approval. "May I serve you?"

H. H. and Evelyn examined the variety of offerings: bread pudding, fruit pie, cakes and pastries of all kinds, and in the middle, Evelyn's favorite, cream puffs praliné.

"Leave the tray," said H. H.

The waiter smoothed out the tablecloth, relighting a candle in one of the pair of table candelabras and arranging dessert plates. At H. H.'s nod, he removed Evelyn's uneaten plate of salad, popped a fresh bottle of champagne, and arranged it in the bucket. Then H.H. waved him out of the room.

Evelyn was sure that neither man realized that she'd had kept her small, sharp salad knife, hiding it beneath the napkin on her lap.

The director pressed a button that blended discreetly with the dining room's striped wallpaper. Evelyn heard a slow *whhrrrrlll* and turned to watch as a door rolled automatically from a pocket in the wall to the opposite wall and stopped. She heard a click and knew that she was locked in the Hotel Astor's private dining room alone with H. H. Samson.

And H. H. knew that she knew.

"That's just to make sure that no one interrupts us while we have dessert. Have another glass of champagne, Evelyn. I insist."

As H. H. splashed more champagne into her glass, Evelyn said, "I read your script as soon as it was delivered. I saw immediately that it was written just for me, and you can't know how much I appreciate your kindness. But—"

"It *is* written for you. Which is why it's titled *Her Eternal Shame.* Nothing in the story is about revenge. Nothing." H. H. reached into the center of the dessert tray, grabbed a cream puff and plopped it on his plate. "*Her Eternal Shame* is a great title, by the way. Everyone at the studio agrees with me." He pointed his fork at Evelyn and pulled his chair closer to hers. "You really think you can play a girl of fourteen? With those circles under your eyes?"

Yes, Evelyn had been much too excited about the possibility of *Her Sweet Revenge* to get her beauty sleep on the train from Pittsburgh last night. But even though she would be twenty-eight this year, the cameras loved her still. Newspaper reporters still pursued her, curiosity hounds still begged for her autograph through the mail, and men and women still sent her flowers and chocolates—and horsehair whips. Her chin was strong, her eyes were piercingly violet, and she still knew how to feign admiration for powerful men. Yes, she could portray herself at age fourteen.

H. H., on the other hand, had heavy, lifeless bags under his eyes and needed a fresh shave and some Macassar oil on his hair. Now that she was so disagreeably close to him, every fat freckle on his bald head irritated her.

"Maybe we should bind your breasts to make you look younger." H. H. lunged at her, covering her breasts with his beefy hands and grinding his palms into her nipples. "I've seen those advertising photos of you when you were a girl. Even then you had a pair of big ones, didn't you?"

Evelyn pushed his hands away, but gently, as though she were disciplining her child.

He laughed and attacked his dessert with new vigor. As he shoved the pastry into his mouth, Evelyn wondered how big *his* breasts were.

The director gulped from his champagne glass. "I remember those girly advertisements. And those magazine covers! *Cosmopolitan* and *The Delineator*! That's when you first started, wasn't it? Seducing men and making trouble for them?"

On her lap, Evelyn punched the tip of her salad knife into her napkin, feeling the soft threads give way. Working a small hole into the linen boosted her confidence momentarily. She wondered how long it would take her to tear the long tablecloth into shreds.

"If I could only tell you the storyline for *Her Sweet Revenge*, Mr. Samson, I'm sure you would—"

"I was at your trial, did you know that? I had to fight to get into the courtroom; everyone wanted to see the lovely

Evelyn Nesbit Thaw take the stand. And I took notes of your testimony. Here—" H. H. dug into his front coat pocket, retrieving a single page of folded paper. It was dark and well worn at the edges, as though he had unfolded and read and refolded his notations many times since the trial in 1907.

Evelyn looked past the paper to the low candelabra in the middle of the table. How she'd love to see every word on that paper burn.

"It's here, your testimony from court." The director smacked his lips as he spoke, and Evelyn tried to believe he was merely enjoying the last of his cream puff. "It's time to let the rest of the world see your shame. I'm going to distribute this picture to every theater that I can; I bet they'll love it in Europe, I don't care if there's a war over there."

Evelyn forced down a frown. Would her salad knife be long enough?

"Tell me one thing." H. H. pushed the paper back into his pocket and took out a gold cigarette case. "You testified how Stanford White strapped you on that red velvet swing. But did he use the horsehair whip on you *before* he made you sit?" H. H. smacked his lips, and this time Evelyn knew exactly why. "That's what I would have done. I'd have really made you squirm."

* * *

Evelyn Nesbit had been thinking about getting even with her abusers ever since she was a child of thirteen. Ever since the afternoon when a photographer had rubbed her nipples to erection before taking a photograph and then made her wait silently on a stool while he developed the images. And then forced her inspect them as she sat in his lap.

Every day since then, Evelyn had thought about exacting some type of revenge—some type of humiliation or suffering—upon that photographer. Even his death did not diminish her grievance. He was only the first of a long list of men who had rubbed and exposed, groped and jammed, whistled at and fingered her as she tried to make her living as an advertising model and chorus girl.

But the train trip from Pittsburgh yesterday set Evelyn's anger on a new path.

It was only a story overheard, one friend telling another as they sat with their backs to Evelyn's back in the Ladies' Club Car. A story about two boardinghouse neighbors, a man and woman, who roomed next door to each other.

"For weeks," whispered the woman seated directly behind Evelyn, "he sought to attract my attention. And for weeks I deflected each effort gracefully. And then one day, just as I passed him on the stairwell, he turned and snatched at me from behind. He grabbed me around the waist. I lost my balance, and my books fell down the stairs."

"Oh, no!"

"I could feel him against me, feel him throbbing against my skirt. I was terrified. I looked around, but no one else was nearby. I started to yell out, but he put his hand against my mouth. I couldn't breathe!"

Evelyn heard the two women shift closer to each other in their seats. Eager not to miss a word of the story, Evelyn also leaned closer.

"I kept pulling away from him." The woman behind Evelyn whispered so low that Evelyn had to arch her head against the headrest to hear. "I tried to grab the handrail. But he yanked me backwards and cursed in my ear. I teetered on the stairs, trying to reach the railing as he kept pulling me up to his room. We fought each other for—it must have been minutes!—before I heard a door open on the landing above. He loosened his hold—just for a second—and I tore away. I fell forward on the staircase. My skirts swirled below me, and I couldn't see where to put my feet. I fell down to the bottom. When I looked up, he was gone."

"You poor dear!" her confidant exclaimed. "What did you do?"

"I packed my trunk the next day and moved out."

"But what about *him*? What did you do about *him*?"

"What could I do? Even if I went to the police, it would be his statement against mine, and you know they'd believe his. But before I left, I went to the kitchen and borrowed a long knife. The landlady let me into his room, and while she stood there, I took the knife to his clothing. I slashed his pants to shreds and punched holes through all of his hats."

"The landlady let you in? She let you do it?"

"Yes, she did. She'd had complaints about him for months, she said, but her husband wouldn't allow her to throw him out. He and the boarder knew each other; had gone to school together. But when I admitted to her why I had to move out—she almost forced me to tell her—*she* suggested the idea to me. *She* admitted that she'd been fantasizing about doing something like that to him for a long time."

The confidant could not keep down her excitement. "You ruined his pants and hats!"

"I did!" she said, her voice lifting with pride. "Every single pair! I would have started on his collars and cuffs, but I couldn't stand to be in his room any longer."

"Good for you!"

"Yes, good for me! It was a very small revenge, in all honesty, but still, it was very sweet."

Evelyn heard a waiter announce himself loudly at the women's table and their conversation ended abruptly. She knew instinctively that the story was ended—what else, really, could be shared?—but then, as the women stood up from their seats, she heard the confidant whisper, "But if there's ever a next time, I suggest using the knife directly on the bastard. "

* * *

"I won't dignify your comment with an answer, Mr. Samson, but here's what I will tell you: you've got the wrong ending to your picture." Evelyn tapped her finger on the point of the salad knife, which still lay on her lap. Yes, it definitely felt sharp enough. "That woman in your picture is a heroine! She'd never kill herself, and she'd never leave her son to be raised by her deranged husband's family!"

H. H. opened his gold cigarette case and selected a cigarette for himself. He appeared to consider for a second whether he should offer a cigarette to Evelyn. But no, he snapped the case closed.

Evelyn did not need a cigarette; she was already smoking hot. Her emotions blazed as she decided that H. H. Samson was now her captive. The door to the Hotel Astor's public dining rooms might be locked, but Evelyn now possessed the narrative key that she needed.

"I'll tell you how the picture should really end, what today's female audience really wants! In the fourth reel, the husband escapes from the mental institution. He gets a gun and finds his wife and tries to kill her and their son also. He thinks that he can escape his shame as a brutal husband and absent father if he kills them, and so he shoots at both of them. But he misses."

The cigarette H. H. Samson was attempting to light went limp between his lips.

"There's only one way that this picture should end. In the last reel, the husband surprises her in the kitchen while she's cooking dinner for her child. When he shoots and misses once more, she grabs a long kitchen knife and shoves it into his heart. He's dead in an instant."

"Dead?" asked H. H. as though no villain had ever died in a moving picture before. "He dies?"

"Oh, you can give the husband a death scene to increase the drama. He can clutch his heart and look at her and fall to the ground and look up at her again. Then he dies. Women will like that ending, too."

But not for the first time, Evelyn Nesbit had miscalculated how much she could get away with. As she stared down H. H. Samson, expecting his agreement, expecting him to blink, she could read the truth in his eyes. Evelyn would not get anything that she wanted: no change in title, no death reversals, and no starring role in the moving picture of her own life. She was painfully certain that H. H. Samson was still determined to get the thing that prompted the luncheon invitation, and that thing was Evelyn Nesbit.

She would need to use her salad knife after all.

Or could she scream for help and get away? What would happen if she pressed the button on the wall? Would the door open automatically? Would the waiters enter immediately? And would they even help her escape? Or would they ignore her pleas?

But Evelyn took too long in her deliberations. In one monstrous move H. H. pulled her up and bent her over the edge of the table, crushing her chest and face into the white tablecloth. The small gold cross she wore jabbed into the flesh just below her heart. She smelled chocolate frosting and crushed raspberries. She wanted to throw up.

But her knife had fallen to the floor.

Through watering eyes, she saw that only one candelabra remained upright and that only one candle remained lit. She spread her arms slowly along the cloth, her fingers seeking anything that she could use to fight back.

This time, she'd kill the bastard.

H. H. Samson held her down with one hand, pushing her chest deeper into the table. She heard him unzip his pants. Evelyn gritted her teeth and readied herself for the shock. She'd often thought that she was past feeling the pain, suffering the shame, but each time she was wrong.

The director gasped, a deep groan unlike any sound Evelyn had heard before. She braced herself harder against the table, her fingers still stretching for any weapon they could find. His hands lifted from her hips, yet Evelyn's posture remained tense.

As she felt him retreat slightly, Evelyn's fingertips touched a candle that had popped out of the candelabra. Her fingers coiled around the slender, warm cylinder. She'd never stabbed a man with a candle before, but she was sure she could do it. She was also sure that forcing that stick of warm wax through his trouser opening would be sweet.

She felt the weight of his body slacken and heard him bump into the dark wall. She backed away from the table and turned to face him, brandishing the candle between his quivering chest and nether regions.

But his hand was already at his chest and his palm flattened against his heart. The other hand dangled by his trouser opening.

The director reached out to her slowly, his hand creamy with his own excitement. He lurched toward Evelyn and tried to push her aside. She stood firm.

Evelyn suspected that he was trying to reach the button that would re-open the door. She pushed in between him and the wall, spreading her shoulders back and lifting her arms outward to make herself as large an obstacle as possible. She lowered the candle, brandishing the tip of the candle toward his trouser opening. She might not need to shove it in—a revelation that disappointed her—but she could keep him from being rescued by others.

H. H. Samson crumbled to the floor.

She waited minutes until finally touching his jowly cheek with the back of her hand. She felt only cold sweat and stiff stubble, but could hear him inhale and exhale, if only slightly, and she knew he was not dead. Not yet.

Evelyn dropped the candlestick on the table and extracted the folded paper that Samson had shown her from his front coat pocket. She dipped the pages into the flame of the single remaining candle. The paper burned to ashes, which Evelyn blew toward the director's chair.

Before she touched the button on the wall, before she watched the waiters attempt to rouse the director, and long before she gave her statement to the police, Evelyn considered her glass of champagne.

The bubbles were as flat as H. H. Samson's shallow breaths.

She emptied the liquid contents at the director's feet and then reached for the fresh bottle in the champagne bucket. She filled her glass and raised it to her lips.

A solitary glass of champagne was exactly what Evelyn Nesbit needed to celebrate the beginning of her sweet revenge.

* * *

Ana Brazil is author of the historical mystery *Fanny Newcomb and the Irish Channel Ripper* (Sand Hill Review Press) and winner of the Independent Book Publishers Association 2018 Benjamin Franklin Gold Medal for Historical Fiction. Ana earned her master's degree in American history from Florida State University, has worked as an architectural historian, and is now writing fiction full time. Her heroines are independent American women of the late 19th and early 20th centuries who worked smart, fought hard, and persisted always. Her historic ghost story "Mr. Borden Does Not Quite Remem—" is a podcast on *Kings River Life*, and her story "Kate Chopin Tussles with a Novel Ending" appears in the *Fault Lines* anthology from the Northern California chapter of Sisters in Crime. After many years in the South, Ana lives in Oakland, CA.

Stepping on Snakes

by Madeline McEwen

F ifty years ago, Celeste, we were bosom buddies. You hated my insect menagerie and loved my Russian nesting dolls. I hated your coin collection and loved your Siamese cats. Our differences didn't matter until the moment they did, and after that you never spoke to me again.

I wonder why I didn't tell anyone about that day, but I never did. I wish I'd told my dad. I wish I'd told my mum. I wish I'd told anyone, but I never found an opportunity. Seen but not heard—no one ever listened to seven-year-old kids, and nobody ever asked.

* * *

Every day of my childhood in Cape Town, nestled beneath the majestic Table Mountain, was bathed in sunshine, even in the rainy season. South Africa, our new home, banished the memories of our old life in England. I lived without fear, bold and endlessly curious, with a new set of unknown boundaries.

The hours at school were long and dull, but they finished by noon, and the rest of the day I'd ride my mother's sturdy iron-framed bike, hunt giant tortoises in the long Gongoni grass, and collect silkworm cocoons from the mulberry bushes around our garden.

At home, modesty was encouraged but not enforced. I knew what private bodies looked like. I had two brothers, one in nappies and the other in manly boxer shorts. Shame resided at Blessed Benedict Academy, a girls-only primary school in Rondebosch. I didn't fit in because I was boisterous, easily distracted, and asked too many questions, stupid questions.

We wore pale pink uniform dresses with white piping around the cuffs and collar, and a decorative button platen from neck to waist. Why couldn't we wear trousers? Trousers were best for playing tag, riding a bike, and climbing trees. Adults considered these uniforms adorable. I didn't. My purpose in life was to destroy those prissy pink dresses as frequently as possible by accident. I had four hours every day to achieve that goal.

"Grass stains!" my mother would wail. "Not again?"

"Don't fret the child," Dad said with an easy smile.

"Why are you so clumsy, Bobbie? How about some ballet lessons, like Celeste? That girl has such grace and poise."

Dad chuckled, but I fled from the room. I wouldn't be seen dead at a ballet school even if I got to spend more time with my best friend. Why couldn't I take a karate class or judo?

Mum found my report card crushed in the bottom of my satchel. My list of faults was lengthy, far longer than I had imagined: spelling appalling, handwriting abysmal, arithmetic substandard, fidgeting, inattentive, and running in corridors.

"An F!" my mother sobbed. "Your sister's never failed anything. And Harry, he's a straight A student."

I picked the edge of a ragged scab on my elbow.

"That's because F is for funny," Dad said, "right, Bobbie?" He smiled at me, a warm, comforting smile. "They make running in corridors sound like a crime."

"Don't encourage her."

"For God's sake, she's just a child."

"Stop picking, Bobbie. Go take a bath and wash your hair. How do you get so filthy so fast?"

My parents rarely fought. Knowing I'd caused a fight made me shrink.

In the echoing, tiled bathroom, I sat in a couple of inches of tepid, brackish bathwater. The tank was rusty, and mine was the last reluctant bath of the evening.

My sister barged in to use the toilet.

"I can't wait any longer."

I pulled up my knees and turned away. Modesty must be managed. Over the years I'd seen every member of my family in their birthday suit one way or another—practicality overruled privacy in our tiny home, and I barely blushed. I drew a lion's head on the windowpane, sliding my finger through the steamed-up glass. I would be a better student. I would try harder. I would not get an F again.

By the following day, I had forgotten. I burst into the playground at break time and sucked in lungfuls of dusty air with the tang of drying veldt, vast areas of treeless grassland.

I dashed toward the trickle of a creek at the edge of the chain-link fence enclosing the school's grounds. Fences like these were commonplace in Cape Town. They didn't make us safe. Nor had they stopped the German Shepherd from next door at home when he broke free from his tether, leapt over the fence, and took a bite of my bum. But he was only doing his job. Afterward, he looked sad. His owner, a man in a suit, hit the dog with his briefcase and hauled him away, trailing his magnificent bushy tail in the dirt.

Several girls joined me to finger-paint the mud into caveman monsters and tick-tack-toe boards in the dirt. We shared licorice and gobstoppers, sticky and sweet.

The shadow of an adult fell over our games.

"Come away from the perimeter."

Miss Van der Knaap spoke in a thick Afrikaans accent. She wore her thin hair wrenched back from a broad forehead into a tight knot at the nape of her neck. Other teachers relaxed at break time, but Miss Van der Knaap was always on duty and had favorites. She liked girls who had blonde hair and clean fingernails, like Celeste. I knew Miss Van der Knaap didn't like me. She said I was "an unnatural child." But I loved natural things: frogs, tadpoles, centipedes, and chameleons. I looked at my friends and pulled a face.

"What's the *perimeter*?" I asked.

"*Opstand!* Don't be insolent. Keep away from the fence. You girls should be skipping on the playground, not mucking about in the mud like filthy piglets."

I pouted. We were on the right side of the fence, the inside, not the outside. What was the point of a fence? I wished there were no fences, nothing to stop us from exploring, scampering away, escaping into the pallid trees and rough brush to run and roll and frolic like the springboks, the antelopes with their lithe, fluid movements and their signature white flash tails.

After school, I walked with Celeste toward the bus stop. The rolled brim of her hat shaded her face from the sun, but I stuffed mine in my satchel. I hated the itchy straw and the elastic digging into my chin.

Celeste, still wearing her lacy white school-approved gloves, offered me a sweet from a paper bag.

"Want one?"

I'd lost my gloves on the first day, as well as all the other pairs Mum bought.

"Thanks."

I took an aniseed ball because they lasted the longest, maybe until we got home, and they weren't Celeste's favorite.

Leaning against the bus stop pole, I saw a group of boys from Saint Stephen's Academy, my brother's school, rumble up the road toward us. The boy in front, tie askew, rammed me aside and pinched Celeste on the bottom. She howled in surprise and pain. She dropped her sweets and turned beet red. Tears spurted from her eyes. The other boys jostled and fought for the sweets like hyenas on a carcass.

"Pick on someone your own size!" Outraged, I kicked the bully in the kneecap and shot a fist at the bag, volleying it into the gutter. "Get out of here before I give you a dead-leg."

On another day, a week later or maybe a month, teachers huddled on the playground. Adult conversations were usually boring. However, off radar and with free rein, we girls could froth while the teachers chat-chat-chatted in rapid Afrikaans in their private bubble. They loved to gossip, and I always listened. That's how I heard about the illegal marriage between a white South African man and a non-white woman in Bloemfontein.

I also learned that remaining quiet meant we could do anything unseen and unheard: whisper stories, play hide and seek, truth or dare, and my favorite, secret spies. Learning to speak

Afrikaans was mandatory and a daily lesson. I knew the name of every animal in the country, like Olifant, Wildsbok, and Sebra, and the ice-cream seller's slang: *domkop*—dummy—and the bus driver's curse, *misbruik*—pervert. I asked my big brother Harry what pervert meant, but he just laughed and called me a *domkop*.

At the weekend, Dad drove us all to the white sands of Muizenberg Beach for a day of fun and surfing. Harry stripped off his T-shirt and preened like an ostrich with outstretched wings, showing off his muscles.

"You're so vain, Harry." I stuck out my tongue. "You look a tomato, all red and blotchy, like a snake shedding its skin."

"You need to toughen up." He flicked a towel at me. "Sunscreen is for sissies and babies."

I noticed he'd changed shape, no longer a lanky beanpole. His top half had turned into a triangle, wide shoulders, narrow waist. Skipping his share of the chores and a dose of sunscreen, he grabbed his board and hit the surf before we'd unpacked the car.

Hidden behind draped towels, my sister and I changed into our swimming costumes. Gusts of wind tugged at the towels, and we squealed in mock modesty, while Dad hammered on the striped windbreak's poles, driving them in deep. Mum chased my naked little brother, Jamie, to the water's edge and wrestled him into his swimming trunks. Slathered in sunscreen, we swam and splashed under a cloudless blue sky.

Other families began to pack up and drift toward their cars. but Dad liked to stay and watch the stunning sunsets on the horizon, savoring every drop of sunshine. Sometimes we'd stay longer until the sky turned black, stoke up a bonfire, and cook the best sausages, with crispy skins, charcoal flecks, and spurts of greasy juice. But not tonight.

"Can't we stay a little longer? Please, Dad?"

"Nope! Go and rinse off," Dad said.

Mum gathered our belongings, shook the sand off the blanket, and packed away the remains of the picnic. A greedy seagull stole a curly sandwich, drier than cardboard, and swallowed it whole, the triangular crust visible through its bulging neck feathers.

I trudged across the beach toward a single corroded standpipe at the base of the dunes. I stood on the concrete slab near the metal grill covering the drain hole. I flipped on the shower. The first sun-warmed gush was followed by a blast of ice-cold seawater. Sand and stickiness trickled down my legs and arms. I listened to the water glugging into the algae-clogged drain. I wiggled my toes. Then I saw Dad running toward me, shaking his fists and yelling. He never yelled, never raised his voice, never wore that angry face.

"*Voetsek!*" he shouted. "Get the hell away from her."

He wasn't yelling at me. I saw a half-dressed man charging through the swaying dune grasses, bare-bummed. His shirt flapped above his scrawny, hairy legs as he bounded over the mounds and disappeared behind a dip.

I stared after him. I knew I'd done something wrong, but I wasn't sure what. I felt a flush of guilt on my cheeks.

"Damn it, Bobbie." He wiped his brow on his forearm. "You must be more watchful. Aware of what's around you."

"I am aware. I spotted a Cape sugarbird. And I heard a hoopoe squawking a couple of minutes ago."

"Birds aren't dangerous. Some people are. You didn't notice that man creeping up on you? Not everyone is your friend, Bobbie."

"He didn't do anything bad."

"Now, listen to me. You must keep your eyes open. It's not like home. I mean...here, people are poor, starving. This beach is only for rich white Afrikaners."

"We're not rich and we're not Afrikaners."

"No, but we are white. We have to follow their rules while we're in their country. We're only guests."

He draped a towel over my shoulders, swaddled me into a package, and lifted me into his arms.

"Geez, you're getting big, or maybe I'm getting old."

I grinned.

"Older than dirt, Dad."

On the long drive home, with all six of us packed into the car, I entertained myself by peeling strips of dead skin off Harry's sunburnt shoulders. He dozed, resting his head on the window. Occasionally, he swatted me like a lazy mosquito. We were all tired and sluggish in the heat.

Halfway home, Dad pulled in at a rest stop and parked. I bolted from the car toward the rondaval—a traditional round house with a circular thatched roof like a hat—and the toilet. Inside I found three oddly shaped porcelain troughs attached to the curved wall. I pushed the door to the stall. Locked. I crouched to peek underneath and saw a pair of mud-crusted boots astride the toilet's pedestal.

"Hey!"

I turned to see my dad silhouetted in the doorway.

"You're in the men's room, Bobbie. Didn't you notice the sign? Girls are next door, you silly goose. What was I just saying about paying attention?"

I avoided the bedraggled roller towel trailing across in the dirty floor of the women's restroom. I dried my hands on my shorts, hoping Mum wouldn't notice. When I emerged, she was sitting on a blanket with Jamie on her lap and a bottle in her hand. Darn it! Now we'd be hanging around for ages, trapped in the heat until he was fed and burped and changed.

I darted out of sight before anyone had the chance to give me "something constructive to do." Perhaps I could find a river, wade in the water, and catch fish. Wandering into a field, I scanned the horizon. I remembered a watering hole, as black as oil, from our last camping trip. Was that near here? The boys had gone swimming. I wanted to swim too, but girls weren't allowed.

I used my stealthy spy techniques to follow them and watched from the branch of a tall yellowwood tree. My brother Harry and his teenage friends, all shapes and sizes, some as tall as Dad, had plummeted into the water. They dive bombed and skinny-dipped for the whole afternoon. I was quiet, and they made so much noise hooting and hollering that I remained undetected. When they toweled off and lounged around on the rocks drinking beer, I decided not to tattletale to Dad. I was no snitch but a professional spy in training, camouflaged to blend in with my surroundings, my chest hugging the bough, my limbs flaccid like the vines tumbling from the tree. Then I cautiously hunted caterpillars until it was time to drive home.

Once, when we'd first arrived in Cape Town, I'd collected a bucketful of different caterpillars, all colors, all sizes, all busy and wriggling and beautiful. I had gathered leaves to feed them and put them in a cardboard box with breathing holes punched through the top. That night, after I'd gone to bed, I awoke with my hands on fire—the skin taut, fatter than boxing gloves, pockmarked with white pinhead blisters. I'd learned my lesson. Caterpillars' hairs were a warning to humans—don't touch.

Celeste would never have done something so stupid. She didn't have brothers and sisters who dared and teased her.

Dry air filled the late afternoon. I found a stick, poked the undergrowth, and raked the leaves. Where were my furry little friends hiding? I crawled under a shady bower knotted with twisted, gnarly creepers and trailing tendrils. I spotted a gorgeous caterpillar, a Cape lappet with tufts of ginger hair along the sides of its body. It inched its way along a half-eaten ragged leaf. I resisted the temptation and retreated.

"Bobbie!"

I ignored Dad. I wasn't ready to go home. A dust cloud followed in my wake, rising high and spreading wide. I skipped further away into the brush, and the field narrowed and funneled into a potholed track lined with rickety posts strung together by a chain-linked fence topped with barbed wire. I shuffled my shoes and dragged the stick through the dirt with plumes of dust trailing behind me like a steam train. Dad could find me easily if he wanted to.

"Bobbie!"

Dad was getting closer. He sounded cross and not in the mood for hide and seek. I saw something up ahead coiled in a rut in the road and ran to investigate. The sun beat down, and the track shimmered in the heat. I blinked back a bead of salty sweat trickling into my eye. I saw the snake's head and tail shoot up like bamboo sticks. The snake's tail rattled. I stood still, watching its head twist and writhe. Was it true that rattlesnakes lived near water? Snakebites were poisonous. Snakes could kill. Never touch a snake.

"Bobbie!"

Dad was behind me, his voice steady and firm.

"Walk backward, Bobbie. Throw the stick to your side to distract his attention."

I did as I was told. He scooped me up and jogged all the way to the car. He didn't scold me or smack me. He didn't say a word until he put me on my feet when we reached the edge of the rest stop.

"Don't say anything to your mother. I'll explain later. Okay?"

I didn't need an explanation. Mum was afraid of all the new things, the things I found exciting. Cape Town was a long way from home in Plymouth, England. Danger was everywhere, including a whole heap of "political unrest" and "insurgency." I wasn't sure what they were, but I knew they were bad. I found it confusing. Why couldn't everyone go everywhere? There were too many rules. Why were people called black or white or colored when my sunburnt brother was red all over?

I sat in the rear seat of the car with the windows wide open, pinned between my sulky sister and my bulky brother. Jamie, the smallest, slept on my mother's lap until we reached home.

Another Monday arrived far too soon, with more dreary lessons and not enough play time. I watched the red second hand judder around the clock face, each tick taking forever, while waiting for the lunch bell. The lazy ceiling fan droned in slow circles, and I felt my eyelids grow heavy in the heat. Finally, chair legs scraped the floor, and the girl at the end of the last row left her seat to ring the hand bell.

Instantly awake, I tore away from my desk and stormed outside. Celeste and two other girls, my friends, were hot on my heels. We scrambled down the steep bank at the far side of the playground and down to a clearing near the perimeter fence. This spot was ours, our den. We had flattened out the surface, filling the hollows and breaking down the humps until we had a hard-packed arena. I pulled my bag of marbles from my pocket, knelt, and dumped them out in front of me. Celeste smoothed her pink hair band, held out the skirt of her perfectly pressed uniform, and sank gracefully to the ground. The other girls took their positions, and we played rock, paper, scissors for who was to start.

Celeste won. She opened a drawstring bag of her best marbles, ones with the brightly colored spirals encased in glass. Knuckles down, she flicked her first marble. It hit the Aggie, the biggest marble, dead center, knocking it out to the boundary. Each girl took a turn, all intent on winning.

None of us noticed the man until he spoke.

"That's a good game," he said.

He stood on the other side of the fence, close enough to touch—an old man, older than Dad, with a scraggly beard. When he smiled, I saw his long yellow teeth.

"I have a good game too."

His fingers curled around the diamonds of the wire fence. His short nails were dirty.

"Do you like pets?" he asked Celeste.

"I do," I said.

"What about you?" He kept his eyes on Celeste. "What's your name, you with the lovely flaxen hair?"

I gave her a nudge—*don't tell him, you ninny*—and glared at her.

"Celeste," she said.

"Celeste!" I said. "We should go."

"That's a pretty name for a pretty little girl. Do you like pets?"

"Yes," Celeste said, "I love pets. I have a cat named Frank and a guinea pig called Furter and two dogs called Hamish and Hildegard." She licked her top lip and wrapped both arms around her body. "What do you have?"

"Shut up, Celeste."

I shoved her again, but she shoved me back.

"I bet you got the cat first," he said. "Am I right?"

"Yes," Celeste said. "How did you know?"

"I know everything." His weasel eyes darted up the bank and into the playground. "I know about pets too. Things that your parents and teachers don't know."

"What things?" Celeste said.

"Shut up." I punched her arm. "Let's go."

Nobody moved except me. When I stood up, my eyes were level with his raggedy buttonless shirttails. He was taller than Dad, much taller.

"I've got a pet that nobody's ever seen before," he said. "He's rare and beautiful and precious."

Celeste squealed with excitement and leaned forward. I slapped her on the top of the head, not hard, but enough to make her scowl at me for a second before she snapped her attention back to the man.

"Can *I* see it?" she asked.

"In here," he said, making a big show, pulling his trouser pockets inside out, peering at his armpits, searching under his shirt. "Where's he hiding, I wonder?" He undid the zipper on his pants, reached inside, and let his penis flop through the diamond wire. "Here he is. My friend Charlie." He stroked the flesh on his side of the fence. "Say hello, Charlie. Charlie wants to be your friend, your best friend."

I looked at Celeste's face, wide-eyed, open-mouthed, frozen in place. My friends stared. One giggled. No one moved.

"Who wants to stroke Charlie? Celeste, do you want to go

108

first? Here, give me your hand, and I'll help you."

She couldn't, could she? She wouldn't, surely? Celeste raised her arm, hand shaking, fingers trembling. I jumped on her. She screamed as I knocked her flat.

"Don't be such a dumbbell, Celeste."

I grabbed her wrists and pinned them to the dirt.

"You're the dummy," she said, tears spurting from her eyes. "I hate you. You're a rotten friend."

I heard a metallic ping from the fence and swift, soft footfalls through the brush. Then feet pounded across the playground, and someone yelled, a teacher, several teachers.

"That wasn't a snake," I hissed, "that was a—"

I felt hands on my shoulders, and someone pulled me off Celeste.

"*Bullebak!* Bobbie! What a wicked girl you are!" Miss Van der Knaap grabbed me, holding me as tight as a bear even though I wasn't struggling. "What are you doing to poor Celeste?"

I glanced at the fence, through the fence to the field of gently swaying grasses. The man had gone.

Another teacher helped Celeste to her feet, wiped the tears from her eyes, and dabbed her nose. She tenderly stroked Celeste's hair, sympathy and concern etched on her face. The teacher led Celeste up the slope to the playground and onward toward the nurse's office.

Miss Van der Knaap dragged me up the bank, one hand gripping my arm and the other pinching my earlobe.

"I'm taking you to the headmistress, you vicious little heathen. Pretending to be so high and mighty with your English accent. Fake! Fake! Fake! You're far more poisonous than a Cape Cobra."

* * *

Celeste, that incident is as clear today as it was back then. I never meant to ruin our friendship. I only wanted to keep you safe. Now we're older and maybe wiser, do you think we could be friends again?

* * *

Madeline McEwen is a Navy brat from the UK and spent a number of blissfully happy years at the Naval base in South Africa. She settled in San Jose, CA in 1995 and has acclimated perfectly apart from her English accent. She has published numerous short stories in a wide variety of magazines and anthologies, both in print and online. The bulk of her work is in the cozy-mystery genre, with a few non-fiction pieces and a couple of LGBTQIA steamy romantic capers, but always emphasizing the hidden humor in daily life. Madeline is bifocaled and technically challenged. She and her Significant Other manage their four offspring, one major and three minors, two autistic, two neurotypical, plus a time-share with Alzheimer's. In her free time, she walks with two dogs and chases two cats with her nose in a book and her fingers on the keyboard. You can find her at www.madelinemcewen.com.

Women Who Love Dogs

by Dayle A. Dermatis

There is nothing better than being greeted by a dog that loves you. They wriggle from shoulder to tail and back again, as if their joy, their adoration for you can't be contained, as if the uncontrollable motion keeps them from bursting apart in a flurry of fur and pure trusting devotion.

Vanessa Sheridan buried her face in Merlin's fur, not caring about the doggy smell or the slight oiliness in his soft fur. Her whole world shrank down to this moment. He stilled at her touch, as if realizing she needed to hide her tear-stained face in him, and leaned his solid body gently against her crouched form.

"You heard?"

Brooke's voice was muffled, nasal. Vanessa knew she'd been crying.

Vanessa sighed, letting a bit of the tension out of her shoulders, then stood and closed the door of the small ground-floor apartment she shared with her sister, a year and half younger than she. Closed it against the sheeting rain that had made her midnight drive home from the newspaper a white-knuckled one, closed it against the evils of the world as best she could.

"I did," she said.

Brooke had turned on every lamp in the room against the rain and darkness. The brightness was almost too much, adding to the headache vibrating out of Vanessa's tight neck muscles. It drove away the shadows but didn't hide the familiar, comforting flaws.

The clumps of dog fur at the corners of the scuffed hardwood floors, persistent no matter how often Vanessa vacuumed. The barely better than college furniture, mismatched but comfortable: a dark blue oversized easy chair; a blue, burgundy, and green sofa in a pattern best described as "dated"; an antique oak coffee table that Vanessa had refinished in high school, which had taught her she hated refinishing furniture and would never do it again.

The rolling walker with the small black seat, crouched next to one end of the sofa like a four-legged metal spider.

Vanessa sat next to Brooke on the sofa, and Merlin jumped up and laid down on the other side, resting his head on Brooke's skinny thigh. He wasn't an official service dog—the MS hadn't progressed so far that Brooke needed constant care—but he'd had some training, and he was smart and devoted.

"It's all over Twitter, and it was on the eleven o'clock news," Brooke said, grabbing Vanessa's hand. Brooke's skin was cold, dry.

"It's why I was late tonight," Vanessa said. "I had to copyedit the story before it went to press." And she'd had to keep it together, fight to stay calm and professional when all she wanted to do was scream.

The latest victim in a string of rapes up and down the Southern California coast had been identified as their friend Camila Hernandez.

Camila had been their classmate at Ventura College—same year as Vanessa, both of them two years ahead of Brooke. Vanessa clenched her fists, just as she'd been doing the whole drive home, wishing she could have somehow been there, somehow have helped.

"If she's up for it, maybe we could visit her tomorrow?" Brooke asked. "She'd love to see Merlin." Camila had gone on to veterinary school, and Merlin was one of her patients now.

"We'll call tomorrow and see if she's up for visitors," Vanessa said. "I'll have time before work."

"Sounds good." Brooke managed a trembly smile.

Brooke didn't need this kind of stress. Vanessa gathered her into a hug. She'd promised her parents she'd take care of her sister. Promised herself. No matter how hard she tried, she couldn't protect Brooke from this. But she could keep it together in front of Brooke, be the strong one.

Merlin, of course, having heard his name, rested his head on Brooke's thigh. A moment later, though, he wedged his wet black nose between them, breaking up the hug.

"Yes, it's time for your walk," Vanessa said. She was exhausted emotionally and mentally, and her warm, dry bed sang a seductive siren call, a counterpoint to the constant waterfall of rain. But when you had a dog, you had to walk it. The rare rain made it more of a burden than its normal pleasure.

They'd had to find an affordable apartment that was on the

ground floor and handicapped accessible. Ventura, California, had hills to the north and the ocean to the southwest. Brooke needed flat ground, and the closer you got to the beach, the higher the rents. One too many requirements; something had to give, and that was the yard. They had a tiny cement patio edged with decorative rocks and a few scattered succulents.

"He had a play date today, so he shouldn't need much more than a potty break," Brooke said.

"Small blessings," Vanessa said. She dug an umbrella out of the tiny front closet, grabbed Merlin's leash from the hook by the door. Once more unto the breach.

"Be safe," Brooke called as Vanessa went out.

The rain was cold, and the air had a strange cast to it—when you lived in the desert by the ocean, anything more humid than arid was unusual. Streetlights wavered, pressing against the darkness, obscured by the sheets of rain.

Still, Vanessa didn't feel afraid. She had Merlin, for one thing. For another, in each of the eleven cases, the rapist was the one with the dog. Every victim had spoken, at some point in the preceding days, to a man walking a dog.

The problem: each victim described a different man, and each victim remembered a different kind of dog.

Witnesses rarely got all their facts straight. Everyone knew that. Ask ten people who had just seen a car accident what kind of car and what color, and you were going to get answers ranging from a two-door to a sedan to an SUV, and from red to blue to black.

The victims agreed that the man was of slender-to-medium build and average height. They disagreed on hair color and style, eye color, and facial hair. They agreed that the dogs were on the larger side and friendly. They disagreed on color, fur, and breed, although several had said "mutt" or "some kind of mix."

Now Merlin trotted over to a fire hydrant and relieved himself, unconcerned with the rain. She'd have to dry him off before he got the chance to shake himself when they got back.

It felt better to think about mundane things: drying off the dog, grabbing a quick shower, making a quick shopping list for the Farmer's Market tomorrow. Better than thoughts of work and men who attacked women and Camila.

* * *

He's walking on the beach, mid-afternoon. He's calling himself John this time. A bland, common name: easy to remember, easy to forget. The sand is damp and dark and packed from the rain, which finally eased up a couple of hours ago. Random clumps of slimy strands of seaweed have washed up. Everything smells of brine and fish. Clouds scud across the sky, but there are patches where the sun can get through, golden light streaking down to kiss the ocean beyond the pier. The clouds glow as they cross the sun, as if God is watching.

He lets the dog off the leash. It runs at the low waves, barking, then races back. John finds a stick and hurls it, and the dog, true to its doggy nature, chases, grabs the stick in its jaws, returns.

He throws the stick again, this time aiming it to intersect the path of a female jogger. The dog abandons the stick to greet a potential new friend. The woman stops and ruffles the dog's fur. The dog dances around her slender runner's legs.

John strolls casually toward her while she's distracted, making it look as though he's just walking down the beach.

She looks up. Her caramel-streaked hair is in a ponytail, but wisps have escaped, fluttering in the ocean breeze. Her cheeks are pink and her eyes are bright from her run. "Hi," she says with a breathless smile, both from the exercise and, he can tell, from petting the dog. "Is he yours?"

"He is," he says. "I call him Chowder."

It's not the dog's name; he's forgotten the dog's name, actually. No matter. Chowder is adorable, especially for a dog in a seaside park. They all say so.

"What an adorable name," the woman says.

He has a list of equally adorable names that he swaps out regularly.

"Thanks," he says. He keeps his hands in his windbreaker pockets, his shoulders relaxed. Casual. Unthreatening. Today his wig is dark blond, in a rumpled, could-be-a-surfer style. His contacts are blue, and he's let just enough five-o'clock shadow show.

"Hey, are you a dog person?" he asks. "I'm new to the area and looking for a good vet."

This one is a dog person; she has two Papillons at home. She tells him about her vet, and he asks all the right questions.

She doesn't realize how much she reveals in a few short moments of conversation. He's a dog person, trustworthy.

And she has approached him. She has said hello first. She has shown interest. That is the important thing: she has approached him.

"Well, I've gotta go," she says. "Bye, Chowder. Bye, Chowder's dad."

She takes off down the beach. He's careful not to watch her. He throws the stick for the dog again. He really is a dog person. That's how he found out how much women loved dogs, how

116

women found men with dogs approachable.

He is startled, thrown off, when he hears her voice close by. They never turn around, not at this point.

It excites him in a way he's never felt before.

"Hi, sorry," she says breathlessly. "I think my ring fell off when I was petting Chowder. Do you see it anywhere?"

Chowder runs unhelpfully around their feet as they look until John tells him to sit, which he does, mouth open and smiling, panting up at them as they kick through the sand.

"Well, damn," she says finally. "It was my class ring. That's what I get for wearing it when I'm working out. Thanks for trying."

She takes off again.

John sees it as an amazing sign. She approached him *twice*. Surely she won't reject him later.

Not like the others.

This one is different. Special. She could be the one for him.

* * *

"Something's wrong with Merlin," Brooke said.

"He was kind of listless on his walk this morning," Vanessa said.

"He threw up—and it didn't look like he'd been eating grass," Brooke said, as though she was struggling not to cry.

Brooke didn't need added stress.

Vanessa knew the last few days had been hard on her. Visiting Camila had been draining. Their friend had tried to smile, tried to welcome them into her parents' home where she was staying for a while. But every time Vanessa and Brooke stopped talking, Camila . . . faded away. Lost herself in the bad memories.

Brooke's MS symptoms were flaring up, too, thanks to the heat. The rain was gone. Even though Ventura normally stayed twenty degrees cooler than the Valley and LA, the Santa Anas were blowing—scorching, arid winds that came over the desert to the east, sucking the moisture out of everything, making you feel as if you were being mummified from the inside out.

They took Merlin to the local emergency vet, where Merlin even managed a few wags of his tail at the white-coated tech who took him back to be X-rayed.

Brooke flipped through a magazine, clearly not reading any of it, and Vanessa worried at a hangnail, thinking about Camila, until the tech returned with Merlin and the vet.

The vet was a small, bald man, although he looked strong enough to heave a Newfoundland onto the examining table if he needed to. Behind his wire-rimmed glasses, his blue eyes were kind.

"Good news," he said, shoving the processed X-rays into the clip at the top of the display lamp. "See this here?" He pointed with a ballpoint pen bearing the clinic's logo. "Looks like ol' Merlin swallowed a magic ring. It's small enough to pass through him normally; he'll be back to himself in about two days. He might throw up again once or twice—that's normal—but if he's in any greater distress, bring him back in."

The emergency vet visit wasn't cheap, but thankfully it didn't break the bank, either. Brooke did accounting for a number of different nonprofits in town, allowing her to work at home, and Vanessa's editing job was solid. They'd be fine.

And right on schedule, Merlin passed the ring.

"Yippee," Vanessa muttered as she wrapped her hand in a doggie disposal bag and picked the glinting silver out of the soft poop, breathing through her mouth so she didn't have to smell it. She shoved the plastic-wrapped ring in the pocket of her jean shorts and picked up the rest of the poop to toss.

Merlin sat and grinned at her, tongue hanging out, tail thumping against the grass.

"Well, I'm glad you're feeling better," she told him. She flung the tennis ball she'd brought along, and he bounded after it.

They were at one of the seaside parks, a big grassy area ringed by a concrete jogging and bike path. Little kids with helmets firmly buckled on their heads pedaled their tricycles with grim concentration. On the other side of the path, past the sandy volleyball area, ice-plant covered dunes rose toward the clear blue sky. They blocked the view of the ocean, but not the smell of wet and salt.

Over by the covered picnic tables, a trim blonde personal trainer was putting three students through their workout, having them step up on the concrete benches, do a squat, step down, do a squat, and then do it all over again. Vanessa's quads burned in sympathy.

Keeping one eye on Merlin, Vanessa bent and turned on a low tap outside the stone bathrooms. It was designed to let people wash the sand off their feet before they headed to their cars, but she always found it useful for filling Merlin's travel bowl. She stuck the ring under the stream until it was no longer poop-covered, then she wiped it approximately eight million times with paper towels.

She'd assumed it would be one of hers or Brooke's. She was wrong.

It was a class ring from Santa Clarita High School. When Vanessa saw the inscription, she felt a wash of cold run through her despite the heat. Bile washed up into her throat.

The name on the inscription had been released to the media last night.

Jessamyn Dupree. Twenty-two. College student, bartender. Latest rape victim.

* * *

John is astounded and furious. Why did Jessamyn reject him? She approached him twice. Twice. That showed clear interest in him. An obvious desire for him.

But in the end she turned out to be just another cock tease, another fake. He waited for her after her shift at the bar, offered—like a gentleman—to walk her home, but then she tried to dial 911 surreptitiously on her phone.

Normally he leaves town after his ordeals. Rents another dog, tries again. But he's been rattled by this one. He's angry—no, he's livid. He doesn't want to wait this time.

He wants to try again to find *her:* the woman who will accept him, love him like he deserves.

* * *

Officer Ortiz led them in to a small room, empty except for benches on either side. The gunmetal gray doorway was narrow, and it took a long moment for Brooke to maneuver her walker through. Ortiz looked uncomfortable, as if he were making a mental note that the problem needed to be fixed.

Vanessa made sure Brooke was settled on the wooden bench before she sat. The bench was hard and uncomfortable, and the room smelled of cheap air freshener and the body odor the spray was supposed to cover up. Officer Ortiz sat across from them. His uniform looked too big, as if he'd lost weight recently, although he looked fine for his lanky frame. His dark mustache was trim, his hair buzzed.

He held Jessamyn Dupree's ring in a clear plastic evidence bag.

"Where do you think your dog was when he ate the ring?" he asked.

"We're not entirely sure," Vanessa said. "It must have been near our apartment—I walk him twice a day. I didn't see him eat it, though."

"He's also signed up for Rent-a-Pup," Brooke said.

Officer Ortiz raised his eyebrows.

"It's an online service that rents dogs to other people," Brooke explained. She was looking a little better, a little stronger in the air-conditioned station. "Golden Retrievers need to get out and run. It's hard for us to give Merlin that, so we signed him up. We pay an annual fee, and so do people who want to rent dogs."

Ortiz shook his head. "I'm not sure I get it."

"There are people who love dogs but can't have one for some reason," Vanessa said. "Maybe they're in an apartment that doesn't allow pets, or someone in the house is allergic, or they work really long hours. It's their chance to spend time with a dog."

Ortiz might not have been up on the latest sharing economy schemes, but he wasn't stupid, either. "So you think the person who rented your dog raped Jessamyn Dupree?"

"His name is John Flynn," Brooke said, fishing a printout from her purse. "Here's the application he filled out. He came to pick up and drop off Merlin. He has blonde, shaggy hair like a surfer and blue eyes. I don't remember anything else specific about him, though." She hunched her shoulders. "He seemed nice," she added, her voice thin.

"If he paid with a credit card, we can trace it," Ortiz said. "Thank you, ladies. Because of you, we may just be able to nail this sonuvabitch. I'll call you if we have any follow-up questions."

But it was Vanessa who called the police station again the next morning, asking for Officer Ortiz. Doing everything she could to keep her voice from shaking, she told him that through the Rent-a-Pup website, they'd received another request from John Flynn to rent Merlin again that day.

* * *

John senses something is wrong as he approaches the too-quiet apartment.

The anger grows inside him like the rising tide. What has the skinny girl with the walker done? Has she rejected him too? He doesn't want her, not in that way. But if she's like the others, she should pay.

He likes her dog. He didn't think someone with such a nice dog could be such a betraying bitch.

He knows he should turn, walk away, but it may be too late. Then he'll have to spend so much time explaining why, explaining how it's their fault, how he's only punishing them for accepting and then rejecting him, for leading him on.

And his rage at the skinny walker girl is a red wash across his vision, like when you lie on a hot beach with your eyes closed and the sun tries to pierce your lids.

He practices his easy smile. Drops his shoulders. Tucks his hands casually in his jeans pocket.

Wraps his fingers around the knife.

* * *

Vanessa understood what Merlin must have felt after he'd eaten the ring. She wanted nothing more than to throw up, then curl into a little ball with Merlin, just like she'd done when she was sad as a kid and snuggled with their beagle, Sparky.

There had been no time to set up an undercover officer. no time to figure anything else out. If they had delayed in telling John he could rent Merlin, they would have run the risk of losing him.

So she stood in the living room with the mismatched furniture and dog fur in the corners of the wooden floor and waited for the doorbell to ring.

Brooke was around the corner in an unmarked car with Officer Ortiz. Safe. That was all Vanessa cared about. That and stopping the rapist from ever hurting another woman again.

When the bell rang, she nearly screamed. She could smell her own acrid sweat, knew her shirt was damp under her arms. Merlin sat on the sofa where she'd told him to stay.

Her hand was shaking so hard she almost couldn't flip the deadbolt or twist the knob.

He pushed his way inside so quickly that she was forced back, away from his closeness. He wasn't a large man, and she wasn't a small woman, but his presence was overpowering.

The blank look in his eyes. They were brown. His natural color or contacts? It was a stupid thing to wonder. Anyway, her world was focusing down to the knife in his hand.

"Where's the skinny bitch?" he asked, eyes flicking past her.

"The one with the walker?"

Vanessa didn't know how to respond. Dimly she heard someone shout, "Police! Freeze!" and the man—John—the rapist, grabbed her arm and pulled her hard against him...and then Merlin made a noise she'd never heard before.

She knew the growl he made when he saw a ground squirrel or gopher.

This growl was nothing like that. This was terrifying—and yet somehow comforting.

Merlin launched himself from the sofa and over the coffee table in a leap she'd never imagined he could do. John shouted and held out the knife, but Merlin landed and sank his teeth into the man's leg. John yelled in pain and let go of Vanessa. As she fell to the side, she saw the knife come down, and then she heard a very, very loud bang that reverberated and rang in her ears even after it was over.

* * *

John loves dogs, and he doesn't understand why the dog attacked him. John was only trying to protect himself.

Unlike women, dogs never reject him. Until now.

His leg throbs in time with his heart.

* * *

Vanessa pressed her face into Merlin's soft, stinky fur. The man hadn't stabbed Merlin, not in the end. He'd dropped the knife as the police shot, as near as anyone could tell.

Nobody else had been hurt. Everyone was safe. Brooke was safe.

She was shaking again, this time from the aftermath of adrenaline and fear and shock.

But holding onto Merlin kept her from bursting apart.

* * *

Dayle A. Dermatis is the author or coauthor of many novels and more than a hundred short stories in multiple genres, and her short fiction has been included in year's best anthologies in mystery, erotica, and horror. Her thriller story, "The Scent of Amber and Vanilla," received an honorable mention in *The Year's Best Crime & Mystery 2016*, and "Voices Carry" appeared in *Snowbound: Best New England Crime Stories 2017*. "Bothering With the Details" and "Pirate Pete's" have appeared in *Alfred Hitchcock's Mystery Magazine*, and several mystery and spy stories appear in current and upcoming Fiction River anthologies. She is the mastermind behind the Uncollected Anthology project, and has recently branched out into editing anthologies. To find out more, check out www.DayleDermatis.com.

Jewel's Hell

by Lynn Hesse

B ess's feet hit the floor in the next room and stomped down the hallway. Jewel grabbed a plaid flannel shirt from a mound of discarded clothes on the apartment floor, fought to find the armholes, and threw it back on the floor. She ran towards her mother's rage. Bess might kill Callie this time.

"Please. *Please.* I need to go to the bathroom," Callie said as Bess opened the closet door.

"My God," Bess said. Her voice bounced off the thin walls. "You've pissed on the floor again."

Jewel saw her sister Callie wedged into the corner of the closet, thin arms wrapped around her knees like taut twine.

"See, Jewels. Miss Twiggy can't control her bladder any better than she can control her mouth or her *wandering* hands." Their mother poked her head inside the closet.

Callie shrank into a smaller ball. "It's really a shame to see you like this, Callie, but you bring it on yourself."

The girl's dirty blonde hair and beige sweatshirt blended

into the unpainted drywall. Bess was only slinging insults, a good sign, because often her beatings were doled out in sudden strikes. The sight of her younger sister's sunken cheeks and the odor of the filthy clothes stacked on the washer and dryer shot a star of pain into Jewel's stomach.

Bess slapped the back of Jewel's head. "What are you waiting for? Get busy. Clean it up."

Happy birthday to me, Jewel thought as she wiped up the urine with a towel, a greasy wad taken from the top of the dryer. It was best to carry out her mom's orders without thinking. Two years ago on Jewel's thirteenth birthday, the first night Jewel was put out on the streets to earn the rent money, Bess had rewarded her daughter's protests by chopping her hair off and burning her drawings and paintings.

"I gotta pee," Bess said.

After Bess left, Jewel leaned close to her little sister.

"I'll try and sneak you some food when snake woman leaves for the afternoon."

Callie stared into space.

"Like you didn't do yesterday and the day before."

"You're almost thirteen. She's been watching. I know it's been longer this go-around, but you keep yelling stuff. A neighbor might call the police. And you shouldn't of said Dad was smart to leave."

"I found a letter in her cedar chest," Callie said.

"She found you in her room? Oh, God, no wonder she's furious. Why were you pawing through her things?"

"It wasn't locked like usual. The letter was from Papaw. He said Momma *betrayed* him with our daddy."

"Are you sure about that word?"

"B-e-t-r-a-y-e-d," Callie said. "Is that the reason I never

127

knew my daddy?"

"You hush. She was a kid herself once. Papaw had needs." Jewel stroked the side of her sister's head. "Oh, never mind."

"I hate you." Callie pulled away. "And I'm hungry."

"I know. I remember how it was. It will be okay, Callie. She's just mad because Jeff wrecked the car last night. It'll cost her money she don't have. No insurance and all."

Callie thumped her temples as if counting off the seconds.

Jewel closed and locked the flimsy closet doors, blocking Callie's view of the living room. Her sister was in deep doo-doo. She had dug up a family secret Bess considered taboo. According to Jeff, Papaw had valued his possessions, and he had loved Bess "like no other" until he died, a couple of years after Callie was born.

Callie might have a chance if Family and Children's Services found out about the beatings, but the neighbors ignored most noises, and Bess preached that what happened at home should stay at home. "The world don't need to know family business. Don't care anyway."

Jewel planned to take off as soon as she saved another five hundred dollars. She'd strip if she had to. Survive. Her younger sister couldn't go. Extra baggage. Maybe Jewel would make an anonymous call to social services after she got away.

Bess intercepted Jewel as she came down the hallway.

"Go fix me and your brother our breakfast. I'm busy here on the phone with the power company." Bess tilted her cell phone.

Jewel pulled her brown stringy hair behind her ears and headed for the galley kitchen. She couldn't count the number of times the power had been cut off this year because Jeff, her older brother, had needed bailing out of a mess. She opened the kitchen cabinets, looking for the pancake mix. Bess loved pancakes. A good breakfast would put Bess in a better mood, and she might get the hell out and go shopping at the local flea market. Then Callie could eat.

Bess shouted expletives into the phone as she paced between the open living room and the dinette area.

Jewel watched her mother over the kitchen counter as she emptied the milk carton and added water to raise the level to half a cup. Stirring the batter, she calculated the number of days that Callie had been in the closet. Bess had gone nuts on Tuesday and shoved Callie in the closet for being a "sneaky smart-aleck." Now it was Friday. The overburdened school officials might get around to calling about Callie's truancy next week.

Jewel had slipped Callie water each night before leaving for the truck stop. "No water, no mess. But then, no Callie," she muttered as the butter sizzled hitting the hot griddle. The white noise of the neighbor's television seeped through an adjoining wall in the kitchen in between the sounds of Bess railing on at the power company employee on the phone.

"I'm telling you, I paid that electric bill. If your people weren't so dumb, we wouldn't be without lights and heat. We're freezing." Bess took a long draw from her cigarette. "I have a small child and Granny to worry about. How old? My daughter is nine months, and my great-grandmother is eighty-three." Bess put out her cigarette in an ashtray on the kitchen table. "Yes, I've been trying to tell you that I sent that check three days ago. Okay, yes, that's all nice and how do you do, but I still don't have no heat. Your supervisor?"

Bess nestled her behind on the couch armrest. "Fine, I'll wait." She exhaled smoke.

Jewel flipped the pancakes and smiled. Bess could scam better than anyone around. The great-grandmother and baby con worked almost every time, unless the same rep answered the phone. It bought a few days of heat. They'd be warm until the power folks sent their advocate to investigate.

Jewel didn't really see any harm in stealing from a rich corporation—but damn the hassle. She hated being cold too. Luckily the kitchen stove was gas, not electric. When the power had been off, she and Callie had made a pallet on the floor under the opened oven door. But not lately.

Callie had looked so small in the closet.

Jewel scratched at a pimple on her nose. Being cold and hungry would be her fate if it weren't for Callie being Bess's preferred victim. Even having those drunken, fat truckers on top of her, pressing the air out of her chest with each thrust, was better than starving in a closet.

Bess said, "Are you gonna put those pancakes on the table or just stand there staring off in space?"

"Oh, yeah, here they are." She laid the pan on the table, then took her brother's work shirt, draped across the back of a chair, and put it on. "Isn't Jeff up yet? I thought he had to paint with old man Crawley today."

"He's up, but he's not feeling good. I told him to stay home and take it easy."

Jewel closed her eyes and counted under her breath. She imagined gripping the frying pan with both hands like a bat. When she opened her eyes, her mom was glaring at her. Bess threw her hands in the air. "Seems like you have something to say. Say it, missy."

Jewel scanned Bess's arms and stomach pushing against the table. She had thirty or forty pounds on her. Jewel closed Jeff's worn shirt over her slip and locked eyes with her mother.

"Changed your mind?" Bess grinned. "You spineless wimp. The only thing you're good for is done on your back."

Blood rushed up her neck and cheeks while a musty odor of soiled hotel sheets and stale cigarette smoke seemed to liquefy and drain down her throat. She crossed her arms over her breasts. She bathed in scalding hot water, but it was useless. The stench clung to her.

"What do you want to say, princess?"

Jeff stood in the hall entryway several feet from the table, yawned, and scratched his head. Her brother's lanky body leaned on the door facing. It framed him like a figure in a matted photograph. Jewel liked that he favored their long-gone trucker father.

Jeff, Bess's loyal muscle, made sure Jewel never kept much money back from her tricks, and when he sensed his sister's discontentment, he bought clothes and makeup for her. The older prostitutes working the truck stop had warned Jewel to get out quick before Jeff hooked her on drugs. In private moments, Jewel drew Jeff's portrait, and they talked. He fed her the pimp's line about how talented she was.

"You'll make it one day. Be outta here. Leave me and Atlanta kudzu behind and make it big, living the dream as an artist in New York."

"Nothing. I don't have a thing to say." Jewel picked up the pan, swung it close to Bess's huge chest, and circled to the stove.

Bess grunted.

"Wish you had the guts, don't you, princess?"

"No, Mom. How you want your eggs?"

"I want my eggs scrambled like your brain."

Bess slapped her knee.

Jeff kissed Bess on the cheek before he sat down at the table.

Jewel poured the rest of the pancake batter in the frying pan, making perfect ovals.

"Sis, scrambled will be fine for me too, and three of those pancakes. Mom's only kidding. Don't puff all up. It ruins your pretty face."

Jewel cracked an egg and shot her best drop-dead look at her brother.

"Sure had fun last night, Momma. Me and the guys played poker, and I won twenty bucks."

"Whooee!"

"Shut your mouth, Jewel," Bess said. "That's good, baby," she added in her sweetened iced-tea tone. "We'll fix the car when we can. Don't you worry about it. At least you weren't hurt in the accident."

"Thanks, Momma."

"You deserve some *reck-e-a-tion* after painting on your weekends with that old geezer Crawley. You know his one eyebrow kinda makes me think of an ape."

"You're right. It does. You sound just like Crawley. *Reck-e-a-tion*." Jeff stretched himself across the table and swatted his mother's raised hand. "You can always make me laugh."

"I guess we shouldn't make fun of the man." She flopped back into the chair. "Trouble follows him wherever he goes…and he lost his wife last year."

"Momma, you're too much," Jeff said. "Still my best girl."

Bess said, "You remember that the next time your willie perks up at one of those high school girls."

He measured a bicep by wrapping his hand halfway around it. "Don't worry. I'm about to graduate. Since I'll be twenty

132

soon, I'm looking for a real woman like you, Momma."

"Women like me are hard to find." She pulled her T-shirt tight across her breasts and slid a hand over her belly. "Over the long haul, who wants a skinny ass like Callie or Jewel?"

"I don't, but some do. Jewel's been filling out lately. Most senior boys drool when she bounces those tits by them in the halls."

Jewel dropped the coffee pot on the table and plopped on the couch. She glared at Jeff.

"Or maybe word's got around," Jeff said.

Bess pushed Jeff's upper arm. "Watch your mouth, son. Your sister may be for sale, but she ain't cheap. Anyway, her school days are about over. I'm pulling her out next week."

Bess dipped a finger in the syrup on Jeff's plate and licked the tip.

Jewel gritted her teeth. School had been her saving grace, her fantasyland, a temporary stay from home. She had managed to eke out passing grades until high school. She even had a best friend. But Jewel had made the mistake of telling Carol what she was forced to do. "You're a whore," Carol had said and walked away, leaving Jewel to stand alone in the bustling hallway.

She could blame Bess, but Jewel knew she wasn't smart. She struggled to read a paragraph, the words jumbled up in her brain, and math was impossible. She probably would've flunked out soon anyway.

She closed her eyes, trying to block the tears. Besides, during the Christmas break, Bess had got used to the daily income. She decided doing tricks on weekends wasn't bringing in enough money. Jewel started working at the truck stop two or three nights a week, skipping school the following day. She couldn't face the chatter of the "normal kids" in the hallways. How could they understand a brother who lied about taking you to a special place for your thirteenth birthday, drove you to a strip joint, got you high, and set up your first trick in a dirty bathroom?

"Look at this cash." He had spread the bills out like deck of cards. "The guy paid extra because you were a virgin. Mom was right, you'll bring in more money because you can play a cheerleader or the girl next door, at least for a while."

Jewel cried in the backseat as Jeff drove her home. At the apartment he offered to share his bucket of chicken and talk in her bedroom, but she shoved him away and slammed the door.

"Jewel, don't be like that. At least the guy was a businessman in a suit for your first time. Bess wanted me to hook you up with a trucker." She could feel him standing outside her door. Waiting. "I tried to talk her out of it." He jingled the door handle. "Please."

She balled up in her bed in a fetal position and covered her head with a blanket.

He punched the door.

"It's not like you wouldn't be doing it for free soon anyway."

When Jewel was young, Jeff had been the older brother she looked up to, her protector. Their dad had left, leaving their mother pregnant with Callie. They had invented a game, Wibble Wobble, to sidetrack Bess when she flew into a rage. To distract Bess, Jeff would rub her feet or back on the couch—sometimes in the bedroom.

Jewel opened her eyes and watched Bess play with Jeff's curls along the nape of his neck. A cockroach crawled across the table.

During those hours pre-teen Jeff kept Bess happy, Jewel always turned the television up and cleaned house. She learned early on to keep her thoughts to herself.

"Space cadet. Get up and do the dishes," Bess snapped her fingers at Jewel. "We're gonna sit outside in the breezeway and finish our coffee."

Jewel gathered the dishes. She would miss going to her art classes, but she had never belonged; the teachers expected her to drop out. Nobody cared. Only once their half-blind neighbor, Millie, had asked, "Why do you take it?"

"I do what I'm told to do," Jewel had said. "She's my mother."

As Jeff carried in the folding chairs, loud banging came from the laundry closet.

"Jesus, Jeff, go teach that girl a lesson," Bess said. "Use my belt this time, and make it hurt. I mean to have peace and quiet in this house, even if I have to kill somebody."

Jeff fetched the belt from a hook mounted on the kitchen wall and walked toward the closet. The oversized belt buckle had fake rhinestones. He turned the key over in his hand. "What's a squeaky mouse doing making so much racket?"

The door shook from a blow from inside.

"I'm starving," Callie screamed.

"Now, now, little one," Jeff said.

"Don't hit her above the shoulders," Bess said.

Callie kicked the double doors open. As she burst out, one of them walloped Jeff on the forehead. He swayed backward, then stumbled forward.

She pushed him away.

His head hit the hallway door frame hard.

Callie's eyes bulged as she stared at Jeff, dazed on the floor with the belt buckle glistening beside him.

Callie snatched up the belt, wrapped it around her hand, and faced Bess.

"I'm not afraid of you, snake," she said in a shaky voice as a mass of arms and legs stamped towards her.

Before the girl could move, Bess landed a left hook to Callie's jaw. It spun the child around, and her arms flapped like bird wings. She landed on her rear end, losing her grip on the belt. It uncurled as it arched, the heavy buckle spiraling down as it ripped skin from the side of Bess's face.

Bess wiped the blood away.

"You little shit. You're dead. You were a mistake to begin with."

Jeff moaned, and Bess bent to help him.

"Callie, run," Jewel said.

Callie bolted for the door, stumbled over a pair of raggedy tennis shoes, and bounced off Millie, who stood on the stoop, blocking the exit. Callie pushed the old woman aside and ran.

"What's going on?" Millie said.

Jewel slammed the door shut.

Millie pounded on the outside of the door. "You all right in there? Do I need to call the police?"

Jewel felt an icy calm. With Callie gone, Bess couldn't play little sister against big sister anymore. She stepped over Bess's legs as her mother rocked her limp brother on the floor.

"Oh Jesus, I can't lose you too, Jeffrey. Wake up. I need you."

"Call an ambulance, Jewels. Goddam it, where are you going?"

"Be right back."

In her bedroom, Jewel unsnapped her purse while she watched Callie from the second floor window. When the girl reached the street, she hesitated, gazing back at the apartment, and waved up at Jewel.

Jewel knocked on the glass and let her breath fog the window glass.

"Go on. It doesn't matter which way you go. Just keep moving."

As Jewel saw Callie run up Gilmer Street toward The Food Mart, Bess ranted in the other room.

"Ungrateful children will be the death of me. If you die, I have nothing. You hear me? Wake the fuck up."

Jewel dumped the contents of her purse on the bed. The .38 pistol fell out last. Her red fingernails gleamed against the pearl handle grips. Jeff had given her the revolver, early on.

"Take this gun," he said. *"Some of those good ol' boys have mean streaks."*

Bess's voice shook the walls.

"Call for help, or I swear, Jewel Katherine, I'll smash your teeth down your throat."

"And some mothers are mean through and through," she murmured.

Jewel lifted the gun barrel, and in the dim light it seemed to fuse with her long fingers—a blue steel extension of her arm.

She studied the empty street.

"That's it, little sis. Don't ever look back. Hell don't need a witness."

Jewel dropped her arm and cocked the hammer.

Bess's feet pounded on the tile floor toward Jewel.

Jewel felt the winter sun hit her back through the window.

"This is gonna feel so good."

***

Lynn Hesse was the 2015 First Place Winner, Oak Tree

Press, Cop Tales, for her mystery, *Well of Rage*. Her suspense novel *Another Kind of Hero* was a finalist for the 2018 Silver Falchion Award. Her short story about a domestic homicide, published in an anthology, was adapted as the play *We Hunt Our Young*, produced at Emory University. As a police sergeant in DeKalb County, GA, she developed a street unit to deal with domestic violence. After retiring, she worked with women prisoners—many of them in prison for domestic violence related crimes—through Reforming Arts, using InterPlay experiences, and also taught them short story writing. An interview concerning Lynn's role as a police officer, as exemplified in the dance video *Blue Steel*, is in the Women's Studies Archives, The Second Feminist Movement, Georgia State University. She performs for social justice in several dance and theatrical troupes in Atlanta.

Banshee Scream

by Gin Gannon

I can follow the stench of a killer's guilt from a hundred miles away. I'd been tracking this particular scent for the last twenty-four hours. Whoever it was, he didn't sit still for long. I must have logged five hundred miles zigzagging across Massachusetts in my hunt for him.

I was close now, though. I just couldn't figure out what he was doing in a hospital.

I paused to study the map of the building posted on the wall of the lobby. I didn't need directions to find my prey; the scent trail would lead me there. I did need to know where I might encounter obstacles and where I could dispose of the medical waste when I was done. It would also be useful to know where the best escape routes were to avoid drawing undue attention to myself.

A smiling young man in a wheelchair rolled over to a spot beside me. He had a lanyard around his neck with an official card identifying him as a volunteer. "Can I help you?"

No one could help me. That was a fundamental truth of my

existence, one that was starting to gnaw at me. Even a banshee could get lonely after about a hundred years of interacting only with people I would only know for a few hours or days before they died at my hands.

I gave the map on the wall one last glance, noting the emergency exits and the location of the morgue, where a few extra body parts wouldn't be noticed.

"Thanks, but I know where I'm going now."

As I entered the elevator, the stench of guilt grew stronger. It clung to the button for the fifth floor, so that was where I headed. According to the map, I'd end up in a cluster of operating rooms dedicated to cosmetic surgery.

I stifled a yawn while I waited for the doors to open. I'd barely gotten a decent week's sleep after a month of tracking down my last killer. I wasn't at full strength, and it seemed like I was getting weaker and weaker as I was called out to hunt more often.

I hadn't even had time to figure out whose murder I was avenging. I knew someone had died violently, since I'd woken three days ago, only partly restored from my last mission, with a primal scream. It was a warning to anyone who had committed murder that there would be justice. When the sound had died down and I'd filled my lungs, I'd locked onto the stench of guilt that had led me on the path that ended here. I knew a murder had happened, but there hadn't been anything in the news that would explain whose death had awakened me. All the recent reported murders had been tragic but routine, cases the police could resolve without my intervention.

I wished I were wrong about yet another killer potentially evading human justice. I couldn't let that happen. Not again. It would destroy me. A fate I'd accepted when I became a banshee. And yet, I was being called out with increasing frequency, leaving me exhausted and jeopardizing the success of my missions. If this were a false alarm, I could get the rest I needed for future cases. But I knew that wasn't possible. I was never wrong about murder. That knowledge was a basic fact of my existence.

Maybe the body hadn't been found yet, so it was being treated as a missing persons case. Those seldom got much news coverage, unless it was a child or there was something unusual about the situation.

In the waiting room, the scent was strong and unmistakable. It still surprised me that humans couldn't smell it. But banshees existed to spare humans from horrors they couldn't tolerate, disgusting smells being only the least of them.

I didn't resent human obliviousness, but it would make my job simpler if I could go up to the receptionist and say, "Excuse me, but I'm here to take care of that nasty stench for you, if you'd be so kind as to unlock the door marked 'Employees Only' and then completely forget you ever saw me. Thank you for your assistance."

Instead, I had to wait, leaning against the wall next to the employees' entrance, until the door opened and a staff member came out. I stuck a heel in the door to keep it from closing. I stood totally still until the receptionist was called away from her desk. Then I slipped inside my killer's lair.

What was the killer doing with a cosmetic surgeon? Did he think changing his appearance and fingerprints would help him to escape justice? That might work with other humans, but not with me. There never was and I doubted there ever would be a form of surgery that could interfere with my identification of a killer.

The scent of my current prey led me to an office with the name, Edgar Winters, M.D., and his specialty, cosmetic surgery, permanently painted on the closed door. No replaceable signs or shared office space for Dr. Winters.

I listened for a moment, wondering what the killer might be saying to the doctor. If I was lucky, he'd be confessing to what he'd done, although that seemed highly unlikely. These things were never that easy.

I knew he was guilty, just by the stench, but it was traditional to get a verbal confession before going forward with the punishment. In fact, if he expressed remorse and asked for forgiveness, I could turn him over to the police instead of taking care of matters myself, and then I could get back to the much-needed restorative sleep that his act of murder had interrupted.

Despite the fancy lettering of the doctor's name, the door itself was flimsy. I could hear no voices, only the rapid tapping of someone using a keyboard.

I slipped inside to find that the office had only one occupant, a man of around forty in good physical shape. He had wavy blond hair, brilliant blue eyes, and a face with enough character to it that I didn't think it had been sculpted in one of the nearby operating rooms. I realized the killer had to be Dr. Winter himself.

For a moment, I had trouble believing it. A doctor, supposedly dedicated to "first do no harm." Maybe I'd made a mistake. I'd been feeling burned out lately, with too many cases in too short order. But I couldn't be wrong. The distinctive stench of murder-guilt was overwhelming in here. If a killer had left before I arrived, the smell would be dissipating with every second that passed, not growing stronger.

There was only one way to be absolutely sure. Taste his blood. Just a little peck on the cheek or maybe the lip. As long as I didn't breathe in the stench, it might even be pleasant kissing such a handsome face. It had been longer than a human life since I'd last kissed anyone for pleasure.

The killer hadn't looked up from his typing yet.

"Wrong room," he said in a tone that was a great deal less pleasant than his appearance. "This is a private office."

"I'm in exactly the right room," I said. "And you must be Dr. Winters."

He finally looked up, stopped typing, opened his mouth and shut it again. He was reacting to my natural form of camouflage. As long as I willed it, humans saw what they wanted to see. Dr. Winter was seeing a human female who was small and blandly pretty. Only later, when I'd gotten what I needed from him, would he see my real appearance.

"You are a killer," I said, "and I'm here on behalf of your victim."

"Ah, so I had it right originally," he said. "You belong on the psychiatric floor. That's the next one up."

"I'm not crazy." What I was about to do might seem that way to both of us, but it had to be done. Before he could escape, I leaned across the desk and nipped him on the lip, just enough to get a drop of blood.

"You *are* crazy!" he said. "Get away from me!"

I had to stop gagging before I could say, "It might seem that way, but it had to be done."

If the stench in the room hadn't been enough to convict him, his blood was. Not only was it bitter with guilt, it also tasted rancid, as if it had been left on the shelf too long. This told me that the killing had been premeditated. It hadn't been some act of malpractice he'd failed to own up to or some spur-of-the-moment, emotion-fueled fatal mistake. No, he had planned the murder and brooded over it for long enough to rot his blood.

"The blood doesn't lie." I spat the remnants of it into his face before I straightened away from him. "You definitely murdered someone."

"I'm a doctor," he said, wiping off the spit. He sounded more insulted than scared now that I'd backed away and determined to defend his reputation. "I would never kill anyone."

"But you did."

"I'm sorry you think that." His voice took on the tone of someone explaining simple matters to a child or a person with limited mental capacity. "It's a sad fact of life that patients do die sometimes, but that's not the same as murder. You need to accept that. Otherwise, I'm afraid I'm going to have to call Security to have you removed from the building. Neither of us wants that."

I ignored his threat. The arrival of human security guards would be inconvenient, but they couldn't stop a banshee.

I still needed to hear him admit his guilt. "Were there any 'sad facts' in your operating room recently?"

"I'm afraid so," he said, assuming an appropriately sad face that I didn't believe for a moment. "One of my patients died three days ago. She was such a lovely young woman, but she couldn't see her own worth without surgery. And now it's too late for her to understand her real beauty."

He was lying. Persuasively even. A human might have believed him. Not me. I'd been tracking him too long to have any doubts now that I'd tasted his blood.

A banshee never failed. I'd known from the beginning that I

would find the culprit, pronounce him guilty, and carry out his punishment. But one thing still surprised me.

"You killed a patient?" I was outraged. No wonder the stench and the blood were so foul. An involuntary scream erupted from my throat, not part of the mandatory ritual, but a wild howl of anger and despair. "You killed a *patient!*"

"I didn't kill her," he said irritably "She just died. Surgeons aren't gods, you know. Sometimes there's nothing we can do to help. Death is a risk of any operation."

"You killed her, and you meant to," I said flatly. "The blood doesn't lie."

"The hospital investigated and cleared me."

That would explain why I had to take care of him.

"I'm not the hospital."

I let go of the camouflage that had let him see what he wanted to. I only gave him a hint of the real me. He stared, perhaps considering how cosmetic surgery might make me more socially acceptable. I hoped I appeared as scary as I should. I really was exhausted.

"Who are you, anyway?"

"Someone who's offering you one last chance to do the right thing," I said. "All you need to do is go to the police, confess to the murder, and accept your punishment within the legal system."

"Why would I do that? I didn't kill her. No one suspects me of anything, and I doubt they'll listen to anyone without a medical degree."

He was bragging about getting away with murder. Of a patient.

Bragging.

To a banshee.

145

"So, you're not going to take the lifeline?" I said. "Is that your final answer?"

"You're crazy, lady."

"Assume for the moment that I'm not," I said. "Assume that I can, in fact, make you wish you'd never killed anyone, even make you wish you'd signed up for life in prison. Are you willing to take that risk?"

"Melanie was going to ruin me too, and look where that got her," Winters said smugly, leaning back in his chair. "She was coming out of the anesthesia when I went to check on her, and she asked me if she was going to be perfect enough for me now. She wanted me to marry her. Stupid bitch. The surgery was supposed to be my farewell gift to her, the end of our relationship, not the beginning. I'd told her that, but she refused to believe it. And I knew that when she finally did accept reality, she was going to be furious, like it was my fault she'd had some fantasy of a life together. She was the vindictive type too, so there was a real risk she'd report me to the authorities for having an affair with a patient. After everything I'd done for her in the last two years. I couldn't let her have that kind of power over me. And I won't let you ruin me either."

"I always accomplish what I set out to do," I said. "I'm not vindictive, but justice might look that way to you."

"Get out of here before I have to hurt you." He rummaged through the papers on his desk and came up with a scalpel that he apparently used as a letter opener. He stood and shoved it in my direction as if he thought he was strong enough to kill someone who could fight back, someone who wasn't medically sedated. "A doctor doesn't just know where to cut for the greatest benefit; he also knows where a cut can inflict the most damage."

I rolled my eyes. It wasn't polite or in keeping with the gravitas of the situation, but seriously? He thought he could scare me?

I was too tired to put up with this garbage any longer. I didn't have time to toy with him, to make him suffer as he deserved. I needed some rest before I dealt with the next scumbag. "You think you can kill a banshee with a teeny-weeny little scalpel?"

He clambered onto the desk, the scalpel out in front of him, as if he were in some bizarre jousting tournament. I reached up to place my hand over his fist and then bent his wrist back until he dropped the scalpel.

"I'm still waiting for your final answer," I said. "Are you going to accept responsibility for Melanie's murder, or do I have to make an example out of you?"

"Fuck off," he said. "And that *is* my final answer."

"I suppose it's just as well," I said, resigned to yet another delay in returning to my lair. "I haven't had to mete out punishment in a while, and I could use the practice. Most people are smart enough to take the other door, not the one with the tiger behind it."

"Go ahead," he said. "Do your worst."

"You really shouldn't encourage me." My hands began to expand in size, and my fingernails elongated into massive bird-like claws. I didn't bother to camouflage any of what was happening. He deserved to be scared. "You've admitted to premeditated murder. It *was* premeditated, right? You didn't kill Melanie the very first moment when you realized what she was planning. You had to go get supplies first and make sure no one was around."

"Stupid nurses," he muttered. "Always hovering. But a little distraction in the form of another patient getting the wrong medication to set off the alarms, and the nurses were too busy keeping him alive to notice me slipping into Melanie's room."

"Premeditated then, and you're proud of the fact." I did the obligatory scream that pronounced him guilty.

He finally seemed to realize he was in trouble. Outside the room, I could hear shouts and rapid footsteps. I needed to finish this now.

I locked the door behind me, which wasn't easy to do without opposable thumbs. It would be so much better if he'd just accept his punishment from the human authorities. Then he could let himself out of the office and go straight to the police station. And I could go back to sleep.

"I'm feeling extraordinarily generous today," I said, "so I'm giving you one last chance to do the right thing. Perhaps you've found that your confession to me was good for your soul, and you'd like to do some more confessing to a homicide detective or perhaps a newspaper reporter first, so you can arrange to have your front-page picture taken from the most flattering angle?"

"Fuck that," he said.

"So be it." I yawned. The work I had left to do would use up the last of my energy reserves. "But first I have to tell you that it's now my duty to tear you apart, limb from limb."

Winters laughed.

"You're threatening the wrong guy. I know exactly how much force it would take to remove a limb. A puny little thing like you couldn't tear off my pinkie finger, let alone an entire limb."

"Appearances can be deceiving. Let me demonstrate." I straightened out his pinkie finger and gave it a tug, separating the proximal phalange from the metacarpal. Anchoring his hand with my—well, it wasn't a hand any longer, but it served the same function—I gave the finger a twist and then a much more solid tug, and the admittedly messy amputation was done. "I did warn you."

When he stopped screaming, he sucked in huge gulps of air and said, "Holy shit. How did you do that? Never mind. Just stop. You were right. I should be punished for killing Melanie. What do you want? I can give you money. Or a lifetime of free medical care? There must be something you want more than you want to kill me. Just name it, and I'll get it for you, and then I'll retire, never practice medicine again."

I wasn't tempted. A banshee who accepted a bribe was an abomination, and the punishment was far worse than what I had planned for Dr. Winters. Besides, unlike the people he was used to operating on, I was satisfied with what I had, both in terms of my physical body and the more intangible aspects of my life. There wasn't anything I would change.

Except ... a small voice whispered in the back of my head.

Except ... it would be nice to have a friend. And maybe some free time when I wasn't literally either working, sleeping, or eating, so I could find that friend and do things together. We might even find a way to join forces and prevent some of the murders I would otherwise be sent to avenge. It would be so much better if I, and the rest of my race, weren't needed any longer, and we could finally let go of our own guilt.

But, no, that was just a fantasy. None of that was possible, and even if it was, Dr. Winters couldn't make it happen for me.

"Hurry up and make up your mind," he said. "I'm bleeding here, and I need to schedule the reattachment surgery. I'm running out of time."

"You ran out of time when you turned down my original offer," I said. "Now I have to tear you limb from limb." I placed my hands on his shoulder and upper arm, much like I'd held his hand before removing the pinkie finger.

His face didn't look so handsome now, his eyes wide with horror and his mouth open in a silent scream.

"Don't worry," I said. "Most of the rending is just for show and you'll be dead soon enough. It's not like we do this for fun. But we can't go around letting people get away with murder on our watch. I need to dispose of your arms first to make it easier to tear your head off, but you won't feel anything after that."

Dr. Winters managed to remember he had a panic button and hit it at the last minute. It didn't save him, but it did mean that I had to play hide and seek with the security guards and then the state police before I escaped the hospital. I could go places they would never think of looking, so there was no real chance that they'd find me, but it all took time. Time that I didn't have. I'd spent most of my reserves avenging poor Melanie.

Once out of the hospital, I hid in a dark alley to utter the final scream, the one that announced that justice had been carried out. It also sent a warning to other wannabe killers that if they made the wrong choice, they too would have their day of judgment. And they'd better hope it was in a court of law and not at the hands of a banshee.

* * *

Gin Gannon (not-so-secretly also *USA Today* bestselling cozy mystery author Gin Jones) brings her past experience as a lawyer and her ongoing experience as a patient advocate to her intricately plotted storytelling. She can't always ensure justice in the real world, but her characters always get what they deserve, for better or worse. When not writing, Gin quilts, grows garlic, and advocates for patients with rare disorders.

No Outlet

by V. S. Kemanis

"Nine lives. I figure we're both on our fifth or sixth. What do you think?"

Rocky is noncommittal, but Arlene is certain. At 64, she's reached an age where her memories belong to someone else, a woman from a past life.

Sitting in her favorite rocker, cat in lap, Arlene sips coffee and gazes out the window at her front yard. A beautiful spring morning, the dogwood trees in bloom, white and pink. It's Tuesday, the second day of her "weekend," following a Wednesday through Sunday schedule at the hospital. The joys and emergencies of the maternity ward, where Arlene is head nurse, are out of mind for another day.

Beyond her front yard, the street is empty of traffic. The brief morning rush is over, commuters in their late-model sedans and mothers with school children in minivans. A few minutes ago, her new neighbor Cherise walked up the street, returning home after taking her son to the school bus stop. Not even a glance at Arlene's house. Perhaps she forgot

Arlene's open invitation to stop in for coffee—or perhaps she just doesn't care to visit.

Arlene recalls a time when the silence after the morning rush felt surreal, almost scary. A time when she stayed home with her very young children. They'd just moved from the city into their neat white colonial in this bedroom community. After Warren left for work in the morning, Arlene and her two toddlers could have been the last humans on earth, awaiting the arrival of aliens, the *whoosh* of their spaceship at the end of the cul-de-sac.

Now, Arlene loves the quiet, but today she feels a bit sad and edgy. She didn't get much sleep. "Warren, I wish you could see this!" Blossoms and the lush green of early spring are certainly fine to enjoy in solitude, but so much nicer when shared with a loved one. Arlene's adult children, Scott and Marni, are both married, long gone from the nest, and it's been a year since Warren lost his battle with cancer.

She still has Rocky. The cat wiggles down deeper. *More please.* Arlene increases the pressure from head to tail, feeling the bony skull and knobby vertebrae under the fur. The calico surrenders to intense pleasure, his eyes squeezed into slits. He lets loose a loud rattle.

A sudden noise swallows Rocky's purr. A rusty rattletrap disturbs the peace, sputtering at a crawl up the cul-de-sac. Arlene can almost smell that plume of dirty exhaust belched from the tailpipe. In slow motion, like a ventriloquist's doll, the driver's head turns from profile to full face as he passes. At this distance, his features are indistinct. Arlene has a feeling more than anything else. Human eyes, male, are watching her house from behind that dirty pane of glass.

The wreck disappears from view, but the still frame lingers.

The man in that junk heap does not belong here. A dreadful anticipation creeps in.

Two minutes from now, the man will be driving out again, after making his slow exploration and turning around at the dead end. Or maybe he'll stop somewhere further up the street. He's searching for something or someone, that much is clear from his stealthy pace, his strange interest in Arlene's house.

She watches and waits. If Cherise had stopped in for coffee, they would have been chatting in the kitchen, oblivious to the interloper. Out of sight, out of mind—but Arlene knows it's better to pay attention, to keep her eyes open, to remain alert. Inattention can cost too much.

* * *

Arlene met Cherise only a few weeks ago, shortly after she moved into a cottage up the street, a little white dwelling on a flag lot behind a larger house. The people who owned both properties, the Zakharovs, lived in the main house but worked long hours and were rarely seen. They rented out the cottage, which was empty for quite some time before Cherise moved in with her six-year-old son, Buddy.

Arlene didn't notice any moving vans but happened to see her new neighbors on a Monday morning, when she was picking up her newspaper near the mailbox. Glancing up the street, she saw Cherise and Buddy emerge from the Zakharov driveway, on their way to the school bus stop at the mouth of the cul-de-sac. Arlene considered introducing herself right then, but it would have been rude to lie in wait and interrupt them when they were trying to catch the bus. Instead, she paid Cherise a visit later in the day, when the boy was still in school.

154

With a paper plate of homemade cookies in hand, Arlene traversed the driveway along the flagpole strip of the parent lot to the rental in back. At first, she thought that no one was home—the cottage had no garage, and there was no car in the driveway. She knocked and waited, eyeing the dirty-white clapboard façade. Inside the house, fingertips touched the edge of a curtain, there was a furtive glance out the front window, and Cherise came to the door.

"Hello!" Arlene greeted the young woman with a big smile. "I'm your neighbor at number nine. Welcome to the neighborhood!" She held out her offering.

The girl seemed startled and responded with a timid hello. To Arlene, anyway, she was a "girl," 25 or so. Cherise wore an ankle-length skirt of colorful mandala tapestry and leather sandals, displaying unpainted toenails. Thin, mousy brown hair fell past her shoulders, one side pushed behind her ear to reveal a dangling beaded earring. She stood in the doorway of the modest cottage like a poster child for the Summer of Love. They exchanged names and a bit of small talk, and then it seemed best to turn around and go. But before Arlene could move, Cherise surprised her with an invitation to come inside.

Arlene sat on the couch and glanced around the tiny living room. Few possessions, sparse furnishings. She happened to know that the owners rented the place furnished, and it looked like Cherise hadn't added much of her own. No signs of a man. A child-size baseball mitt lay on the coffee table. Cherise followed Arlene's eyes as she looked at it. "I saw you with your little boy, walking to the bus stop. He's a real cutie!"

"Thank you." Cherise looked away. "I don't have a car, so we have to walk. For now." She seemed embarrassed by this.

"Walk to the corner?" There were mothers on this street

who always drove their children the tenth of a mile to the bus stop. What a shame, this aversion to fresh air! "Oh, but it's great to walk! Kids hardly get outside anymore."

Cherise met her eyes and smiled.

"I always used to walk with my kids. I have a boy and a girl, all grown up now, with their own homes!" Arlene gave a little laugh. "I like to see youngsters in the neighborhood again. What's your son's name?"

"Buddy. He's in first grade. A good boy."

"I imagine it must be hard for him, changing schools so late in the year."

"Mm-hmm."

"Oh, I'm sorry! Maybe you didn't have to switch schools when you moved?" Arlene wasn't fishing for information, just making conversation, but it seemed to be coming out slightly wrong. She *did* feel something for this girl Cherise, without quite knowing what it was. An aura radiated from her, youthful sparkle with a bit of hardness. *Stand back. Come closer.* A flavor of loneliness, tinged with wariness or fear. Vulnerability? Perhaps it was only that Cherise felt overwhelmed by the move.

"Well, we did have to change schools. It's been hard."

"I'm sure Buddy will get by and make new friends."

"Yes. He'll have to. He has no choice."

"What school district were you in before?"

"Oh, it was…" She looked at the ceiling in a charade of searching her memory.

Arlene quickly filled the void. "Not easy to uproot and move, I know. It's been many years since we moved here, but I remember how it was, in a new house with young kids. I stayed home with Scott and Marni for a few years, then I started up my nursing career again."

Cherise just smiled, and Arlene felt she'd stayed too long for the first visit. "Let me know if I can be any help. I work five days a week, but I'm off every Monday and Tuesday."

"Thank you."

"I'm glad to give a lift if you need to go shopping. Or maybe Buddy would like to see his friends from the old neighborhood?"

"That's really nice."

There was an awkward moment of silence. "Let me give you my number."

"Okay. I'll get a pencil and paper." Cherise walked into the other room and Arlene glanced around, uncomfortably aware of her desire to know more. No sign of a phone, but there must be a cell phone somewhere. No family photos on display, but Cherise had only just moved in. Two cardboard boxes were shoved into a corner. When Cherise came back, she accepted Arlene's number without offering her own in return.

Having accomplished that single welcome-wagon visit, Arlene had no legitimate reason to go back. Two weeks passed before they met again. On Arlene's Monday off, she happened to be outside at bus stop time, weeding the tulip bed closest to the road. The bus had just let the kids off. A few cars whizzed by, carrying mothers and children too lazy to walk home from the corner. Then Cherise walked up, hand in hand with Buddy.

"Well, hello there!" Arlene stood up. "It's a beautiful day!"

"Yes, it is." Cherise stopped, put her arm around her son's shoulder, and pulled him close. The boy looked up at his mother sweetly.

"Is this your little man?" Arlene was impressed with the child's comfortable submission to maternal closeness. Her own boy, Scott, was already asserting some independence at that age.

"This is Buddy."

"Hello, Buddy! I'm Arlene. I'd shake your hand, but I don't think you want to touch this dirty old glove!"

"Arlene made those chocolate chip cookies for us, Buddy."

The boy's face brightened. "I ate 'em all!"

"I'm glad you liked them. My own son used to love chocolate chip."

Cherise glanced back over her shoulder at the empty street.

"Well, Buddy, let's get you home." Her voice carried a bit of fake cheeriness. "Enjoy your gardening."

"If you'd like, Cherise, stop by tomorrow morning for coffee on your way back from the bus stop! Or any Monday or Tuesday."

Cherise turned around long enough to say, "Thanks, Arlene." Later in the afternoon, Arlene made a trip to the store for some Danish pastries, something to have on hand if Cherise stopped by for coffee.

After dinner, Marni called to talk about a patient. New in her career as an obstetrician, Marni valued her mother's experience and advice. She told Arlene that, while examining a pregnant patient, she had noticed fading bruises that might indicate spousal abuse. She had accepted the woman's explanation as plausible and was now struggling with self-doubt. While discussing the case, Arlene felt her own huge secret stirring within. She'd never told her children the details, only the broadest strokes, a diluted version that had seemed appropriate when they were young. Warren was the only one who had known everything.

After the call, alone with Rocky, Arlene had a difficult night.

She sipped herbal tea, watched a TV sitcom, and read a chapter of a novel—light, easy entertainment. Palliatives. When the silence descended, Rocky's companionship afforded little solace. With the TV turned off, the book closed, her mind still active, Arlene told herself to go to bed, but she dreaded it.

Her intuition said that Cherise was the cause of her unease. Images and thoughts of the girl played in her mind. The little half-hidden house, the meager possessions, the absence of a man, the eyes darting up and down the empty street, the mixture of vulnerability and resolve.

In the stillness of night, it came to her: *Cherise is hiding away, just like Juliette.*

Sweet Juliette wafted into her consciousness, a wispy, diaphanous loveliness. "Don't worry about it," she laughed. "Just, whatever you do, if he happens to show up, you don't know me. I don't live here."

Simple instructions, one nineteen-year-old roommate to another, on the day they moved in together, second year of college. It began with an offhand remark: "There's this guy I went out with. He wasn't very nice." A name was given—"Tom"—nothing else, and Arlene's questions went unanswered. Juliette seemed uncomfortable, didn't want to talk about this man. "We'll just keep my name off the mailbox."

The conversation was over in a minute. There was so much else going on. They were exhausted from dragging their belongings up four flights of stairs to the tiny apartment in that rundown walk-up. Then there were classes and parties and other boys to think about. Weeks later, when Arlene was home alone, the buzzer sounded, and the voice of a stranger came over the intercom, asking for Juliette. "She isn't home," Arlene said. The man went away, and Arlene didn't realize what she'd done, the secret she'd revealed. Worse than that, she never told Juliette about the man's visit.

Months later, through her tears, Arlene gave truthful testimony at the trial, but the judge wouldn't allow her to say what she *knew* in her heart, the tacit messages in Juliette's behavior about Tom, the guy who "wasn't very nice." That selfsame Tom was now on trial for Juliette's murder, and Arlene's intuition was not "evidence." Nor was there DNA evidence in 1975, only blood evidence that didn't rule out thousands of other men. Witnesses claimed they'd seen Juliette with Tom in public places, laughing, apparently enthralled. Of course, this was no indication of his innocence, but the jury bought the lawyer's argument that it created a reasonable doubt. Arlene was sitting in the courtroom when the verdict was announced: "Not guilty"—as if it were the truth.

For three years after that man got away with it, Arlene bottled up her shame and guilt, zealously following a self-constructed road to redemption. She enrolled in a nursing program, got her degree, and worked tirelessly for the sick and the dying. How many good deeds would it take to erase her one big mistake? She met her future husband, a pediatrician, at the city hospital where she worked, and he was the first person to receive her full confession.

"Could the jury have gotten it right?" Warren asked gently.

Arlene clutched her abdomen and shook her head. Nothing could dissuade her that the jury got it wrong.

"Either way, you're not responsible," Warren said. "You don't know if that was Tom at the door when you answered the intercom. Even if it was, you said only three words to the man."

"Three words that told him she lived there. I also knew that our building was a wreck. Anyone could break in."

"You didn't know what kind of person he was."

"I should have known. No! I *did* know. I could see it in the way Juliette was acting."

She couldn't make Warren understand that most women simply know these things—or are destined to learn them—whether the awakening arrives with shocking clarity or gradual disillusionment. Violations, major or minor. Warren didn't agree with her, and it made her mad, until she saw that her anger was misdirected. His logic-based arguments didn't make him an apologist for the bad men of the world. He was the strongest, kindest, most empathetic man she'd ever known.

"I think," he said, "you're confusing what you knew *before* with what you knew *after*. It was a terrible shock the next day, when you came home and found her." Lifeless. Raped and strangled.

But there was no confusion. On their first day together in the apartment, Arlene knew exactly what Juliette was trying to tell her. She just wasn't paying attention.

From that time forward, Arlene vowed to pay attention, to remain vigilant, never to let her guard down. Inattention could cost too much. This resolution became her steady lifetime project, ingrained in everyday existence, just as it gradually pushed down the shock and the guilt. Day by day, she removed herself a bit further from that horrible mistake, the three words that had led the predator to his prey.

* * *

Now, forty-five years later, who's to say that mistake wasn't the doing of a different woman named Arlene, just a girl really, a college student in Manhattan, age nineteen? A girl who didn't know how to pay attention? But this new trick of disowning her memories can't alter the past. These memories belong to Arlene alone. And Cherise has rekindled them.

After a rough night, only a few hours' sleep, Arlene is up early. She makes a full pot of coffee to go with the Danish pastries. Everything is ready in case Cherise stops to visit.

Outside her window, commuters speed by in their late-model sedans. Then Cherise and Buddy walk down the street, followed by the harried moms who drive their kids to the corner. A few minutes later, when Cherise makes her return trip, Arlene tries to discern a slight pause in her step, any indication that she wants to stop for coffee. There is none.

Arlene's disappointment, her fatigue, and Rocky's deep contentment keep her in the rocker a few minutes longer until that noisy rattletrap makes its appearance, sputtering up the street. A car that doesn't belong. The stranger's eyes stare through the dirty glass, and now she can't move from her seat. She's compelled to pay attention to this.

No outlet. He'll have to turn around and drive out again. His return is inevitable—or is it? Will the man stop somewhere further up the street?

Two minutes pass, and here he comes again. He's heading out the cul-de-sac, Arlene thinks, but no, the man wants a second look at her house. His head makes another mechanical rotation.

Now he's slowing down. Now the car is turning into her driveway.

Rocky arches his back, electrified fur standing on end. Arlene grabs his midsection and jumps to her feet, but the cat is having none of it. He struggles and flies from her arms. The driver gets out of the car and stands there, examining the house. Arlene moves to a corner of her window where she can watch him and duck out of view if he comes any closer. He's a young man with a messy ponytail. Now he's coming up her walk, wearing oil-stained jeans and a loose muscle shirt over his tattooed torso. He doesn't look happy. She pulls back from the window just before the doorbell rings.

What is this? Rocky paces at her feet. A warning. Arlene has a choice. She can pretend she isn't home. There's nothing to give her away. Her own car is inside the closed garage and all the doors to her house are locked. She hesitates, and the doorbell rings again. There's nothing, really, to consider, no other option. She refuses to play blind. This man is here for a reason, and she needs to know what it is.

Leaving the chain on the door, Arlene opens it and says, "Hello! You must be with the lawn service!"

He gives her a confused look. "No, I'm not."

"Well then, they'll be here any minute. How can I help you?"

"Is Cherise here? Cher Finley?"

Looking into the man's eyes, hard as brown pebbles, Arlene wonders how on earth he happened to choose her house, out of all the houses on this street and all the houses in the world. *She isn't here.* The wrong words.

"No one by that name lives here."

He scrunches his brow and cranes his neck to look behind her, as if he'll find Cherise just inside the door. "Someone told me she moved onto this block, into a white house."

"*This* white house?"

"They didn't know the number."

He exudes the heat of desperation. She can feel it, and

something else. Volatility. Unpredictability.

"Whoever told you that is mistaken."

She considers telling him that her house is the only white one on the block, but she's no good at lying and doesn't want to give him cause to check up on her. He's already missed the only other white house, the little cottage, half hidden behind the Zakharovs' house. He also missed, by just a few minutes, Cherise walking back home.

He looks at the paneling around her front door, as if to convince himself that this is, indeed, a white house.

"I'm sorry, but you're mistaken."

She starts to close the door.

He utters an expletive under his breath and walks away.

She watches him get into his car and back it out of the driveway, hesitating at the edge. Is he thinking he should take another look up the street? *Go left, not right!* His moment of indecision yields to her telegraphed message. He turns left, heading out the cul-de-sac.

Arlene stands at the window, heart pounding. Rocky paces and stops long enough to yowl in full voice. Arlene yowls back: "To hell with fresh air! Buddy will be getting a ride today." Should they pick him up at school immediately or wait until the bus drops him at the corner this afternoon? They'll decide what's best in a minute. Cherise will know what that man might do.

Quickly, Arlene grabs her purse and keys and heads for the garage. A minute later, she's inside that little, dirty-white cottage, talking fast, describing her unexpected visitor, watching the color drain from Cherise's face.

The girl is too stunned to talk, but Arlene doesn't need to hear the full story. In her heart, she knows enough of it. The rest will come in time. For now, nothing could be clearer. This young woman who was strong enough and brave enough to leave, to protect herself and her son, can't do it all on her own. Not now. That man might come back to the neighborhood, looking for another white house.

Cherise grabs a few things and gets into Arlene's car. They're headed back to the white house where "no one by that name lives." Once they're inside, behind closed curtains and locked doors, they'll talk it over and decide what to do. Together, they'll come up with a plan, and Arlene will do whatever it takes to keep Cherise and Buddy safe.

* * *

V.S. Kemanis—attorney, dancer, choreographer, mother, novelist—has had an exciting and varied career in the law and the arts. She has worked for the Manhattan District Attorney, the New York State Organized Crime Task Force, and the Appellate Division of the New York State Supreme Court, most recently as supervising editor of decisions. She is also an accomplished dancer of ballet and contemporary techniques and has taught, choreographed, and performed in many venues. Publishing credits include four novels of legal suspense featuring prosecutor Dana Hargrove, five collections of short fiction on wide-ranging themes, and stories appearing in *Ellery Queen's Mystery Magazine* and *EQMM*'s *Crooked Road*, Vol. 3 anthology, among others.

A Dog's Life

by Ann Rawson

L iz was exhilarated. Her leap of faith had paid off, and she was the newest support worker with the community youth outreach team. Her interview had gone so well that when she said she'd lived in the area for a couple of months, they'd offered her the job on the spot.

Walking up the hill towards the dirty red brick tenement she now called home, she passed two small children playing in the gutter. Ben, a toddler with an angelic smile, filled a rusty can with dirty water and passed it to Kelly, hardly more than a baby, with a halo of blonde curls. The little girl drank from the can, then spat out, grimacing. Liz shuddered. Rats played in that water.

When she'd moved in just a few weeks earlier, Liz would have dragged the kids next door to Flora, the boy's mother, and tried to persuade her they needed to see a doctor. A week ago, she'd have wiped their faces clean, taken away the can, and given them a plastic cup from her own kitchen. Today, she sighed and walked on, lifting her cotton skirt to avoid being splashed.

For the interview, she'd discarded her usual blue jeans and put on an embroidered cheesecloth blouse, ruffled skirt with lace-edged petticoat, and hand-painted Doc Martens.

The sublet council flat in a dilapidated 1930s tenement building was all she could afford. There wasn't much choice of rental properties in the middle of term, and she couldn't bear to stay in her room in the Hall of Residence any longer.

The whole area, from the football ground to the nearby tower block awaiting demolition, had a reputation for its layabouts and petty thieves. Bad even for Liverpool, people had warned, advising her to use a friend's address on job applications. Luckily, she had ignored them.

She'd been nervous about living there on her own until she met Flora. The day after she'd moved in, she'd been asked round for a cuppa. She had barely settled on the sofa before the kids—twin teenage girls and little Ben—swarmed over her.

"Ben's my surprise baby," Flora said proudly. "He'll be an uncle by Christmas. His big sister is expecting."

The two girls, thirteen-year-olds with long blonde hair frizzed up by the damp weather, sat one on either side of her as she drank her tea from a mug.

"Are you Cat'lic or Protestant?" one asked.

"Buddhist," Liz joked. Then regretted it, as she had to explain.

"Have you got a boyfriend?"

"No," she said.

"Why not?"

"Leave her be, you two. There'll be plenty of time for the inquisition later. Let her get used to us first," Flora said. "Thank goodness for my eldest. She lives round the corner and watches the kids when I go to work. Don't worry. I'm not angling for a babysitter. Even with Eddie away, we manage. My mother-in-law, God rest her soul, had eleven. I don't know how she did it."

Ah, Liz thought, joining the dots. Catholic. Of course.

"Away?" she asked. She felt awkward, but decided it was better to know than to risk putting her foot in it if he was in prison.

"He's working the oil rigs in the North Sea," Flora said. "Two weeks on, then a week at home. I bet you thought he was in prison, right?"

Liz blushed. "No, of course not."

Flora took pity on her embarrassment and offered her another biscuit.

It hadn't taken her long to find out that hardly any of her neighbors had jobs. Some were retired, like the old man in the flat above. Janice, Kelly's mother, had quit her job at the local supermarket to spend all day sleeping—tired from her advanced pregnancy or depressed. Maybe both. A Scottish guy in the next block worked on a building site. A few women, like Flora, worked off the books as cleaners. Everyone, including those few in work, signed on at the dole office every week as unemployed.

Still feeling thrilled with her success, Liz unlocked her front door and carefully bolted it shut behind herself. Then she turned the radio on, dropped her bag by the sofa, and collapsed in a heap.

Her adviser had said she was too young to be a social worker. He meant she wasn't tough enough. She suspected sexism, that he'd judged on her appearance—her small frame and her brown shaggy perm.

"Come back when you have some real life experience," he'd

said.

She'd show him she was more than an airy-fairy do-gooder. She'd been a scholarship girl, and her time at grammar school had left her an outsider with both her working class family and her middle class peers at university.

She already felt at home living here among what a certain person would no doubt call scrubbers and riffraff. The working class area she'd grown up in had been less ramshackle and the people more house-proud, but she still felt comfortable here. Once, she'd loved living in student accommodation, but then Dominic Redmond came into her life and ruined everything.

She'd first noticed him in the dining hall. Most of the students dressed in blue jeans. Redmond's clique were mostly law students, and they dressed as if they were already lawyers. Smart trousers and crisp cotton shirts. The girls wore cashmere sweaters, and the boys, tailored jackets.

She couldn't keep her eyes off him. He was tall and conventionally handsome, but what drew her eye was his confidence. People listened when he spoke. That was the attraction. Liz knew she was trying too hard to rationalize her crush on him.

Although she was careful, more than once he caught her watching him and held her gaze until she blushed. He started to talk to her, while the girls in his clique watched. They felt either sorry for her or incredulous, she thought. Or perhaps that was just her own self-doubt talking.

He asked her what she was studying.

"Psychology," she said.

"Ah, that's why you have the human touch," he said. "And you get to dress like a student."

"I like dressing this way," she said, offended.

"No, I wasn't criticizing," he said, for once a little flustered. "You look lovely."

She warmed to him then. A touch of vulnerability made him all the more attractive. Maybe he's thinking about me as much as I'm thinking about him, she thought.

She tried to put him out of her mind. She fancied him, sure, but he was out of her league.

Then he asked her out, and she said yes straight away, with no thought of playing hard to get. Perhaps that was her mistake.

On the big night, she tried on everything in her wardrobe, finally settling on her usual jeans and cheesecloth shirt. She didn't want to make too much of a first date.

She was relieved when he took her to the local pizzeria so that she didn't feel underdressed.

They'd talked and talked. He'd asked her about her old boyfriends, and she'd told him about her teenage sweetheart, who'd broken up with her when she was accepted into Uni.

"Ah," he said. "Some guys can't handle it when a girl has aspirations."

He'd questioned her further until she admitted there'd been no one serious since. "Just a few one night stands," she'd said, before turning the line of questioning back on to him.

"There's never been anyone serious," he said. "So far."

The look he gave her then made her a little uncomfortable and he backed off and started talking about his family.

"My father is a barrister," he said. "I'm following in the family tradition. You?"

"I'm the first in my family to go to University," Liz said. "But my parents are very supportive."

"You're lucky," Dominic said. "Mine kicked up a fuss when I

170

wanted to do Art at A Level."

"That's sad. You do keep up with it though?"

He shrugged. "My mother was the worst," he said. "Her father was a steel worker, but she made something of herself. She got a place at University, and she's a head teacher now."

Liz liked how proud he seemed of his mother. Maybe they had more in common that it had seemed.

Back in his room, the promised coffee failed to appear. He'd put the latest Pink Floyd album on his expensive stereo, and she'd looked around for somewhere to sit. In the tiny study bedroom, the only chair was piled high with books, so in the end she'd perched uncomfortably on the edge of the bed.

He sat down next to her, saying, "Make yourself comfortable. Try to look as if you're staying."

She laughed nervously. "Where's the coffee you promised?"

Dom pushed her down. "Don't be so naive. We both know you didn't come back here for coffee."

She sat up. "I did, actually."

Later, she thought that was the moment she should have left.

He pushed her down again and grabbed her breast. She was shocked, watching it happen as if from a distance.

"No," she said, weakly, pushing his hand away. "That hurts."

He started to fumble with her jeans zipper and pulled it down.

The expression on his face scared her. Where was the Dominic who had chatted over pizza?

"No. Stop it," she said, pushing him away and sitting up again.

"I'll still respect you afterwards," he said mockingly. He pushed her back down. "You've already told me you aren't a virgin."

171

She'd fallen for his chat-up routine, she realized. He'd zeroed in on her doubts about her background. He'd even used his mum to put her off guard. And it had just been a ploy.

He pushed her down again and pulled roughly at her jeans. She was crying silently now. Why had she trusted him? She felt stupid and dirty and could already imagine what his friends would say about her. She was just another of Dom's tramps.

His hand was now on her skin. Her jeans were tight even with the zipper undone, and he moved to one side, putting all his weight on her knee so that she cried out. His fingers clumsily penetrated further, and now he was really hurting her.

"Stop. That hurts. Please stop."

He took no notice, just carried on probing with his fingers.

"If you cooperate, it won't hurt," he said. "Help me get your jeans off."

She went limp and saw his triumphant expression. She lifted her knee sharply and aimed straight for the balls. While he writhed in pain to the accompaniment of "Another Brick in the Wall," she'd fled his room and run across the courtyard to her own room in the women's block, barely pausing to zip up her jeans in her terror that he would follow her.

Her judgment was so poor—that was the worst part. He hadn't ever seen her as a potential girlfriend. What a fool she'd been to imagine him vulnerable. It was all part of his act. She had been too eager to please. She'd gone back to his room. Who would believe her if she reported it as an attempted rape?

Living in the same building had been unbearable. Every day, he would loom behind her in the queue for breakfast. He'd herd his gang to a table near hers in the canteen at dinner. She'd go to the student union bar and he'd bump into her. He'd spill beer on her shirt— accidentally, of course—then coolly look her up and down, say something she couldn't quite hear, and all his friends would laugh.

Ignoring him didn't work. Liz had assumed at first that he would get bored if she didn't respond. She felt ashamed, as if she was the one who'd done something wrong.

She was in the laundry room grabbing her clothes from the washing machine when she felt a hand squeeze her bottom. She whirled round to see Dom sniggering and the clique looking on. None of them had any dirty washing with them.

"Can't you even do your laundry without group support?" she snapped.

"Oh, she bites," Dom said.

"You already told us that," one of the blonde girls said.

"Did you tell them the truth, the whole truth, and nothing but the truth?" Liz tried to brazen it out. She was not a victim—she could fight back.

"I told them you were all over me, and all it cost was a meal at the cheapest pizza place in town," he said.

It was so far removed from how the evening had gone, a total fantasy. She stood slack-jawed, unable to find words.

"You lapped it all up, everything I told you. All the stuff about my childhood, all my broken romances. I had to dump you. You were so keen, it was embarrassing."

She saw red.

"What is it, Dom?" she asked. "Can't get over the fact that I got away? Hope my knee didn't do any permanent damage."

She regretted it immediately, knowing he would never forgive her for humiliating him in public. Gathering up her wet clothes, she almost ran from the room, with their laughter echoing behind her.

Liz could bear it no longer. She found her flat and moved out of Hall, even though she knew she would get no refund on rent already paid. As she handed the keys back to the housekeeper, she hated feeling she was running away.

Months later, she was still flooded with the shame of it all. Dominic Redmond had colonized her mind, and she couldn't stop obsessing on what she might have done differently. Why hadn't she challenged his lies with more conviction? Why was he the one obsessed and following her around, if she'd been all over him and he'd dumped her? Damn fine lawyers they would make if they couldn't see through a story as weak as his. Every time she heard Pink Floyd on the damn radio, her mind got stuck on the same old track. She had certainly needed an education.

But now this stage of her education was almost complete and she had the job she wanted. She'd taken a risk, but it had paid off.

In the kitchen she set about making a pot of tea and preparing her evening meal. She filled the kettle at the sink, watching the playing children through the window. Then she reached for her wooden board and cook's knife and started chopping onions.

She registered a sudden movement from the corner of her eye.

A rat? She looked out of the window again and relaxed. It was only Rex, the neighborhood's shaggy black-and-tan dog, a puppy who'd grown beyond cute and been abandoned. Sometimes she put a bowl of leftovers out for him, and she knew her next-door neighbor Flora did too. When it was raining, Liz would let him inside, and he'd lie on the threadbare rug, nudging her with his cold wet nose, while she read.

174

Liz opened the back door and saw Rex sprawled by the kids, tail wagging lazily. Ben patted him clumsily on the head. Kelly pulled on his tail. Rex growled, and she laughed and pulled harder. Liz called out, "Don't torment the dog, you two."

She watched for a minute or two more, then went back indoors to her chopping board. She'd started peeling carrots when she heard screams. She ran outside in time to see Rex disappear round the corner. She crouched next to the children, her heart pounding. Kelly, still screaming, was lying in the gutter, her blonde curls and scalp matted with blood.

"What happened, Ben? Did she fall?"

"Rex bit her," Ben said. "Bad dog."

It was a nasty bite.

"Ben, get your mum," Liz's voice was urgent. The boy pulled himself up onto his chubby legs and ran home. Liz bent over Kelly, who was whimpering. "It's okay, Kelly. Hush now."

I must get Janice, she thought, then decided to leave it to Flora, who knew Kelly's mum better.

Kelly really wasn't okay. The wound was still gushing blood. Liz tore off a long strip of cotton from her petticoat. She lifted the child onto her lap, wadded up the cotton, and pressed it against her head.

"Hush, hush," she said, rocking the child. She was trying to calm herself as much as Kelly.

"Jesus, Mary, and Joseph, what happened?"

Liz looked up. Flora, thank God.

"Rex," she said. "She was pulling his tail."

"Shit."

"She's going to need stitches," Liz said. "Does anyone have a car?" She'd lived there long enough to know that finding a working phone and waiting for an ambulance could take

175

forever, and Kelly's need was urgent.

"There's only Ken's heap," Flora said. "And that's on four piles of bricks. It'll have to be the bus. I'll take her." She picked the child up. "Can you keep an eye on the kids, Liz? The twins will be back from school any minute."

"Course," Liz said. "What about Janice?"

"Last thing she needs right now. The doctor said bed rest was essential. Kelly was premature. They almost lost her."

"Best let her sleep then," Liz said. She had her doubts still. What mother wouldn't want to know her child was injured so badly? But Flora knew the girl, and she didn't.

"Try not to let anyone else find out Rex turned on the kid, or the whole neighborhood will be up in arms," Flora said. "It wasn't the dog's fault. I'll round them up when I get back and try to stop them going off half cocked."

When Flora returned, Liz was still in her neighbor's flat. She'd put Ben down for a nap. The girls, full of jam sandwiches, were sitting on the floor watching TV.

"They're keeping her in hospital," Flora said. "Twenty-seven stitches, and they're worried about infection. I've gotta go tell Janice. Can you stay a bit longer?"

"Sure," Liz said.

"The nurse said something about bruises," Flora said. "She said no dog did that."

"Bruises could mean anything," Liz replied.

"Mike should be home by now too," Flora said. "Unless he nipped into the pub for a drink on the way."

Kelly's father, Mike, a lot older than Janice, was considered a hero by the neighbors for standing by her when she'd fallen pregnant.

In less than half an hour Flora returned with Janice and

Mike. They wanted to talk to Liz about what had happened. Several other neighbors had tagged along and crammed into the kitchen. Everyone wanted to be involved. Ken, the wiry old man from upstairs, joined them. The couple from round the corner, Liz didn't know their names, but she knew they had two small, yappy dogs. The burly Scottish guy from the next block.

Liz answered their questions as best she could, but it was hard not to feel defensive.

"Kelly's safe in hospital," Flora said to Janice. "Would you like me to take you to her?"

The young woman started to cry, her mass of auburn curls falling over sallow cheeks.

"I don't like hospitals," she said.

Liz put an arm round her. Janice shrugged her off.

"That dog is a menace," Ken said.

"Rex isn't a bad dog," Flora said. "He's protected our kids from the rats time and again. Why do you think I feed him?"

There was an angry rumble from the men.

Flora refused to back down.

"Don't blame the dog. The children were teasing him."

"Pulling his tail," Liz added.

Mike turned on her.

"Why didn't you stop them?"

"It's not her job to watch your kid," Flora said.

"It's all right for you," he said. "Your kid's okay."

"So's yours," Flora said. "Because Liz gave her first aid and I took her to hospital."

"That dog needs sorting," Ken said. "The kid could be dead."

Janice cried louder.

Flora said, "All right then. I'll call the RSPCA. They'll come

177

and pick him up."

"This is men's business."

Mike agreed with Ken. "Let's sort him then. Make sure he won't do it again."

"I've got a rope," the burly guy said.

"You should be at the hospital, Mike." Flora made one last attempt.

"There's only one thing to do with a mad dog," Mike said.

The men swarmed out of the flat.

"Janice," Flora said, "it's time to stop crying. I need your help."

The girl looked astonished, but the tears stopped.

"Come into the living room. Could you just look after the kids for me?"

Flora patted the tatty brown sofa and looked meaningfully at her daughters. They jumped up off the floor and sat on either side of Janice.

Flora shooed Liz into the kitchen. She opened a can of dog food and tipped it into a washed margarine tub, then rummaged under the sink and found an old leather leash.

"If they find Rex they'll hang him," Flora said.

"What can we do?" Liz asked.

"They're not going to find him," Flora said. "We are." She placed the leash and the dog food container in the bottom of her shopping bag.

Outside, the men were milling around, trying to decide where to search for the dog. They looked suspiciously at Flora and Liz as they came out of the flat.

"We're off to the corner shop for tea bags and biscuits," Flora said. "Anything you want?"

"Just the damn dog," Mike said.

He'll be long gone," Flora said. "You could try down the Scottie Road, by the King George. The landlady feeds him sometimes."

The men all streamed downhill towards the pub.

"With any luck, they'll be distracted by the call of the demon drink," Flora said.

They set off in the other direction.

"We're going for biscuits?" Liz asked.

"We're going to save Rex," Flora said.

She led the way to one of the boarded-up houses due for demolition and put the dog food down in the yard.

"Rex. Rex," she shouted.

The dog appeared immediately, bowing submissively and wagging his tail.

As he started to eat, Flora slipped the collar over his head. He started to buck.

"Hold on to the leash." Flora passed it to Liz and held onto the dog firmly, talking calmly to him until he settled.

"Don't be stupid, Rex," she said. "Here I am, trying to save your damn fool life. Don't make me regret it."

When the dog settled, Flora took the leash back from Liz, and passed her a handful of small change.

"Here you go. Try the phones by the shop first. Here's the RSPCA's number," she dipped into her pocket for a slip of paper and gave it to Liz. "Tell them it's urgent. Number 2, Fairy Street."

Liz had to try two phone boxes before she got through. On impulse, she popped into the grocer's and bought a couple of packets of custard creams. Then all they had to do was wait.

They watched in silence as the RSPCA man pushed a cowed Rex into the cage in the back of his van. After he drove off, they walked back to the tenement building.

"That poor child," Flora said.

"Kelly or Janice?" asked Liz.

Flora sighed. "Both of them, I suppose. That Mike has a temper on him like you wouldn't believe."

Liz wondered again about Kelly's bruises and Mike's temper and the way Janice flinched sometimes when he glared at her.

Back in her kitchen, Liz found the gas still alight under a kettle that had boiled dry and warped. She was lucky it hadn't started a fire.

* * *

Days later, life was back to normal on Fairy Street.

Liz was queuing with a wire basket of groceries in the small local shop. Mike joined the queue behind her, and Liz ventured a small hello, hoping to ask how young Kelly was doing. He looked at her blankly, and embarrassed, she turned away, moving one step closer to the checkout.

She didn't see Janice arrive. She just heard Mike explode.

"What the fuck are you doing here? You're supposed to be at home looking after the kids."

Liz glanced back over her shoulder.

Janice, her red curls greasy and dull, was crying, the new baby in her arms. Her face was streaked with tears of exhaustion.

"Go home," Mike shouted.

"I don't want to be there on my own," Janice said.

"You shouldn't have left Kelly. Do you never learn?"

"She's safe with Flora." Janice sounded sulky.

Mike slapped Janice across the face. Janice stumbled, clutching the baby more tightly.

Liz looked around the shop. Everyone had gone quiet. Everyone had apparently gone deaf and blind too.

"Don't you dare hit her again," she said quietly.

"What has it to do with you?" Mike roared. "Who are you, anyway? Oh, right. You're the girl who stood there while that dog savaged our Kelly."

Liz put the shopping basket down and backed away. Everyone was watching now. Surely someone would step forward?

"You heard my husband," said Janice. "What's it got to do with you?"

A fury rose in Liz.

"I don't care what the fuck you two do in the privacy of your own home," she snapped. "Hit each other. Slap the kids. Whatever. But you will not do it in front of me. Do you understand me?"

"Bitch," said Janice. "Keep away from us." She cradled the baby as if Liz were the threat.

"Let's go home, love." Mike put his arm around Janice, turned and spat at Liz. "I know where you live."

As they left the shop, Liz was still shaking.

Behind her, an impatient woman said, "Are you in this queue, or not?"

"Not," Liz said, abandoning her place in the line but picking up the basket.

"Daft," the woman said, shaking her head.

Liz put all the groceries from her basket back onto the shelves as everyone watched. By the time she left the store, Mike and Janice were nowhere in sight. Liz popped into the fish and chip shop and bought a bag of chips, which she ate hot from the greasy paper on her way home.

She made herself a cup of tea. Then she settled down at the

table with the proposal for her thesis and piles of books and tried to concentrate. Planning to take a year out between first degree and postgrad was no excuse for getting behind.

The sound of every footstep on the path outside seemed magnified. Every time the pipes creaked, she looked up. Something fell to the floor in the flat above her, probably the old man's walking stick, and she almost leapt out of her skin.

What Mike had said couldn't be a real threat, could it? He knew she lived next door to Flora, after all, with just a narrow walkway between their front doors.

All the same, when she went to bed that night, she put her cook's knife under the pillow. It wasn't very comfortable, and she could easily imagine cutting herself on the sharp blade as she tossed and turned in her sleep, so she moved it to the chair next to her bed. The chair would normally be heaped with her clothes but she felt so unsafe she settled down fully clothed, lying on top of the covers.

It made for a restless night. More than once, she got out of bed and prowled the hallway. She didn't know what she was expecting. Until she heard it. Glass breaking. The rattle of the kitchen door latch. It must be Mike. Could she make it to the front door and wake Flora in time?

Mike was a big man but slow on his feet. She grabbed the knife just in case and ran for the front door. He was still blundering about in the kitchen, and at least she knew her flat in the dark.

She'd pulled back the bolt and was fumbling with the lock when her arm was grabbed from behind.

"Let go," she pleaded. "Mike, don't be so stupid."

There was a startled laugh as he let go.

"How many men have you been leading on, then, bitch?"

Dominic fucking Redmond.

She opened the door just as he grabbed for her again.

"Flora," she shouted.

She lurched over the doorstep into the passageway between the flats. He tripped and fell on top of her. The knife clattered out of her hand. She'd forgotten about the knife. How stupid was that? She remembered the feel of his body on top of her last time. How helpless she had felt and how humiliated, even though she had managed to escape. The months of harassment until she had run away, leaving university accommodation early to get away from his constant presence.

She went limp.

"I'm not falling for that one again, you stupid cow," he said, holding her down, his hand across her throat, as he rolled off her, out of range of her knee.

In the darkness she smiled. She swung her arm in an arc, as if she were making a snow angel, until her palm connected with the handle of the knife.

"Flora!" she shouted again.

"Quiet," he said, putting his big hand over her mouth now. Then he pulled her up by the arm and tried to drag her back into her flat.

It was all very well having a knife. But what if you were too scared to use it?

She swung her body around, throwing him off balance. She flung herself as hard as she could across the narrow walkway between the flats and landed solidly and noisily against Flora's front door.

"Flora, help!" she shouted.

"Bitch!"

He got to his feet and rushed at her.

Liz could hear movement in Flora's flat. Not long now. She held the knife up in front of her face.

"I'll cut you," she said.

He laughed as he loomed over her. "You wouldn't have the nerve."

She closed her eyes and lunged at him, slashing downwards. He screamed.

The door opened, and the light from Flora's hall illuminated the scene—Liz with eyes closed and knife dripping blood, Dominic with blood running from his eye and down his cheek.

"What the fuck is going on?" Flora asked.

"He broke in," Liz said. "He's why I moved here."

"She attacked me with that fucking great knife," Dominic said.

Nearly all the neighbors were gathered now, watching. Even Mike and Janice, holding the baby.

"What do you want to do?" Flora asked.

"Call the police?" Liz said. She had to report him.

Mike grunted.

"Not much point round here, love," he said. "They're as likely to blame you as him. Listen to that posh voice."

"And look at the state of him," Flora said.

"I told you," Dominic said. "She attacked me with that bloody great knife."

"I just want him to leave me alone," Liz said.

"He won't come back here," Flora said. "We know what he is."

There were murmurs of agreement from the gathered crowd.

"We look after our own here," Mike said.

"If you go to the cops, pretty boy," Flora said, "you'll have us

184

to answer to."

"Scum like you?" Dominic sneered. "What makes you think the police will believe you over me?"

"Who said anything about talking to the bizzies?" Flora said. "It won't be your face takes the brunt next time. See him off, lads."

She put an arm around Liz and walked her into her own flat.

"Back to bed, kiddies, the show's over," Flora said. Then she took the knife from Liz's hand and washed it carefully, before making sure Liz was cleaned up. And she tucked her on the settee with a blanket and an over-sweet cup of tea. Liz slept.

The next morning she woke up to find her flat locked up and the Scottish guy fixing her kitchen door with a scavenged pane of glass.

"You might want a metal grille fixed on here too, hen. If you get one, I'll install it," he said when she thanked him.

It was results day. Liz took the bus to campus.

In the Psychology building, her fellow students were gathered three deep around the notice board. She ducked into the secretary's office to leave her new address.

She was waylaid by the Head of Department.

"Congratulations on your First," he said. "Don't forget about us when you're looking at post grad, will you?"

As he disappeared through the main doors, she went to check the notice board in case he had her confused with someone else. Even seeing her name up there in black and white, she found it difficult to believe.

Drinking a celebratory coffee in the Student Union afterwards, she overheard the conversation at a neighboring table. She recognized the group of law students from her old Hall of Residence.

"So Dom failed his re-sits," one of them said.

"That's not all. He was in some kind of fight. Lucky not to lose an eye. He'll have an ugly scar."

"Badge of honor for a tosser like that."

Funny, Liz thought. They'd never called him a tosser before.

"He was blind drunk, apparently. No one seems to know where it happened, but the police were called to Hall."

"He'll not be back. So there goes his law degree. He wouldn't say how it happened. He punched the Hall porter too. Disciplinary offense, and not the first time."

"There was that girl, wasn't there? Maybe we shouldn't have shut her down."

That girl, Liz thought. Me, or someone else?

Back home, she was longing to share her good news with someone. Out in the yard, she watched as Ben played in the gutter on his own with a toy car. Flora joined her, and they stood side by side watching him play for a couple of minutes.

"I really appreciate how you all stood up for me last night," she said. "Even Mike."

"Rex is gone," Flora said. "I heard this morning."

"I don't understand."

"No one wanted him. The RSPCA puts them to sleep after two weeks if they don't find a home."

"Oh. Poor Rex."

"Still, it's better than being hanged by a mob. I wouldn't trust that lot not to botch the job, either," Flora said. "Cigarette?"

"No, thanks."

Flora struck a match and lit up.

"Can I ask for some advice?" Liz said.

"You're the one with a brain, girl," Flora said. "What do I know?"

"I was planning to become a social worker. Only I don't know any more if I can do it."

"My God." Flora laughed. "We're your guinea pigs, aren't we?"

Liz blushed.

"It's not like that."

"You'll be fine." Flora gave her a quick hug. "Social workers—well, no one round here trusts them. It's a tough job. But someone has to do it."

"I'm more the academic type. I'm not tough."

"I've seen what you can do with a knife." Flora laughed again. "If you can handle Fairy Street, you can handle anything, anywhere."

"Maybe so," Liz said. "Dominic won't be back, at least. But I think I will get a dog."

* * *

Ann Rawson's debut novel, *A Savage Art*, inspired by her love of textile arts and dark fairy tales, was published by Fahrenheit Press in 2016. She's now looking for a home for her second novel, which features paganism, Roman treasure, and a dysfunctional family. In 2008 her short story "The Tree of Knowledge" was shortlisted for the Asham Award. Although she still thinks of herself as a northerner, she now lives near Brighton on the south coast of England. Ann has worked as a receptionist in the ER, as a cleaner and rent collector, and currently as a software tester and small business founder. She frequently walks on the chalk hills and white cliffs with her husband, and while he solves software problems, she plots her third novel. They are often accompanied by their yowling cat.

Subterfuge

by Julia Buckley

Rockland was an invisible town. It wasn't listed on any maps; it was an island surrounded by land. Everyone knew that girls in Rockland had only a few career options: become some kind of unskilled laborer and be unhappy; get married and be unhappier still; be a hooker down by the Dry Gulch Grill and be miserable; or turn to drugs and be stoned or dead. You could also try to get out, but not many Rockland girls figured out a way to do that.

I aspired to leave town when I turned eighteen, but when I graduated, my father said until I could pay for my own ticket I could damn well work in the family hardware store. He didn't pay me a salary because he said I was getting free room and board. So much for earning my ticket. I told him that he was unfairly exploiting my labor. He scowled at me and told me to stop using fancy words on him. I got a second job working nights at the Twilight Motel, checking in tired or lost travelers or the inevitable guys who picked up the hookers at the diner. It was a dismal job, and I saw a lot of hopeless faces, night after relentless night. A few months in I felt old, used up. I missed taking the bus to the high school where sometimes teachers had asked us to think about big ideas, make big plans. After we graduated, though, we were expected to continue those plans on our own; I realized soon enough that people need help for things like that. They need a network. They need knowledge. They need money.

My friend Tamara hadn't liked high school; she was happy just to hang around with her boyfriend Bill, even though he hit her sometimes. She assumed she and Bill would get married after graduation, but he decided to move to Maine to work on his uncle's fishing boat. He left her a note so that he wouldn't have to tell her in person. She sat around crying for about a week, and then her mother kicked her out of the house, telling her not to come back until she had a job.

Tamara wasn't the self-reliant type. She had expected Bill to make all the decisions, to bring in the paychecks. By the time I realized her dilemma, Tamara had already done the worst: she had gone down to the Grill to sell the one asset she had. She confided in me one day while we drank milkshakes at a tiny restaurant called Trudy's that she was already a regular—at least in the Grill parking lot.

Her face looked dead, and she had lost some weight, but she advised that I should parade around the Grill too.

"It pays good money. I'm saving up, and as soon as I have enough, I can go wherever I want, do whatever I want."

"But you don't even have a plan," I protested. "Get out of there, get a different job. Those guys can get violent."

"It's not a big deal. You could do it, Sophia. It's not like you're a virgin. Just go in there, go through the motions, and collect your pay."

"And go to jail," I said.

Her blue eyes, mournful as a widow's, didn't crease when she let out a dry laugh.

"The cops in this town are our biggest customers."

This shocked me. I certainly wasn't under the illusion that Rockland cops were perfect—I'd seen two patrol officers take booze from teenagers and then drink it themselves in their car, and I'd seen another one step all over the crime scene when someone had broken my dad's hardware store window, shrugging and telling my father that without a security camera he could basically give up on the idea that the perpetrator would ever be found. I'm pretty sure the cops closed the case that day. But soliciting prostitutes? And Tamara was right; I wasn't a virgin. But the sex I'd had in high school was with one guy only, and at the time I was in love.

"No thanks," I said.

"There's one guy who's really predictable. Just comes in, lies down, wants to do it missionary, and then he leaves. Puts the money on the table. He's nice enough," she said.

I wondered if *nice enough* was a euphemism for *doesn't hit me*.

"No thanks," I repeated.

"But you keep talking about getting out of town. This guy pays a hundred dollars a pop. And he likes brunettes. Think about it."

"Where does he get that kind of money? Maybe I'll get him fired from his job for soliciting prostitutes, and then I can apply for whatever it is he does. God knows it's just dead-end jobs around here."

"He's a trucker," she said. "He makes good money, and he loves to spend it down at the Grill."

"Why don't guys like him just find someone and have an actual relationship?"

"He does. He's married. A lot of them are."

"It's not for me," I said.

"What is for you? Do you like working at that crummy motel?"

"No."

"Do you like living with your parents?"

"No, ma'am."

She frowned into her cup; the last of the sweetness was there, and she was trying to scoop it onto the end of her straw.

"Your mom never found a way out, did she? How's she doing these days?"

"Depressed. She sleeps a lot. Then my dad yells at her for not being a better wife. I guess he means maid, because he's always crabbing about housework and stuff. She just wants to work in her garden—it's so beautiful, the one beautiful part of her life. Oh, and he keeps finding reasons to complain about my books. Mr. Saylor gave me some as a graduation present, remember? He had a classroom library that I borrowed from all the time, and he gave me a box full of them. I've been reading through them all, and my dad complains. I should be working instead of reading, he says, or that those 'blasted books' are taking up too much room in our house."

Tamara gave up on the last bit of ice cream and pushed her cup away.

"I miss my teachers."

"Yeah."

I had asked Mr. Saylor what it took to become a teacher. He had told me I would need at least four years of college. He might as well have said I needed diamonds and rubies.

Rockland rocks bought nothing. They were the burdens we carried on our backs, weighing us down, down into obscurity.

Tamara paid for our milkshakes. She took out a wallet full of cash; she was trying to prove that she had made the right choice. I thanked her and told her to be careful.

Back at the hardware store, my father looked at his watch and glared at me.

"You don't get movie star lunches, Sophia. Half an hour, that's all."

"Fine," I said.

I went back to stocking shelves. While I was bent over, a burly guy wearing camo walked past and grabbed my butt. I shot upright and glared at him. He only grinned. He wasn't the first man to grope me in the store aisles. I had complained to my dad the first couple of times. He said he would keep an eye on it. But a week later I heard him talking to a friend on the phone.

"Yeah, the store's doing good. My daughter Sophia works there now, and business has picked up. You've seen Sophia, right? Yeah, exactly. Sales have increased."

It chilled me, hearing him talk that way, especially because he thought he was complimenting me. He thought bragging about the beauty of his daughter meant he was being a good father. He couldn't see that I didn't want him or those strangers looking at me like I was some pretty decoration. I was worth more than they thought I was, and it depressed me that my father wasn't making that clear.

After that I tried to stay vigilant and not to put myself in places where men could reach me. It was a daily challenge. But the motel was worse. My boss, Mr. Scanlon, thought he was being subtle. But he found a million ways to make contact with my body, all in the name of "training."

When he showed me how to use his computer system, he insisted on standing behind me and using the keyboard with his arms over my shoulders. Then he'd say, "Now you try, sweetie." He'd rest his hands lightly on my shoulders, massaging sometimes, while I typed what he had just typed in. The program was self-explanatory, but he had to "train" me to establish his dominance. I guess he wanted to prove that he was smarter than I was, which he wasn't, and to try to cop as many feels as he could along the way.

When he showed me how to greet people at the front desk, he acted out scenarios to "test" my knowledge of what to do in various situations. The worst was when he decided to teach me how to handle a drunk and unruly customer.

"Let's say a guy comes in, and he's three sheets to the wind," Scanlon said. He mimicked a staggering drunk, obviously trying to amuse me.

I forced a laugh, but this was increasingly hard to do. He was not funny; he was never funny, but he thought he was.

"So I'll be the drunk guy, and you tell me how you'd handle him."

I knew what was coming, so I steeled myself. He pushed his way behind the counter, too close to me in the small space.

"Hey, I paid my money. Now why don't you walk me to my room, honey?" He pressed me up against the wall and tried to kiss me; in the process, his hands landed on my breasts and started kneading.

I lifted a knee, hard, and got him in the testicles. He doubled over and moaned.

"That's what I'd do to anyone who touched me like that. Even you," I said.

I was trembling, shaking with something that wasn't exactly fear. For a moment I wondered if it was a kind of power, but I didn't know how to put it into a higher gear. I shoved past Scanlon and went to the front desk to watch for guests. I figured if he was going to fire me I could find a job at some other scummy motel.

He didn't fire me, though. He showed up later, not to apologize, but to say I'd passed the test. He said I was a terrific employee and he trusted me to handle things at the counter. I was sitting at my desk, and he leaned down so that his face was even with mine.

"Come on now, look at me," he said.

I dragged my gaze to meet his.

"You know I had to test you, right? You know that needed to be done."

I stared at him, folding my arms against my chest.

"You are a tough one. That's what makes you a great employee." He leaned in and kissed my cheek. "We're going to be the best of friends."

Then he pretended to have just noticed what I was wearing—a T-shirt and jeans.

"Oh, we do need to talk about your wardrobe."

"Why?"

"This is a service industry. We like to maintain a professional demeter."

"Demeanor?" I asked.

His eyes narrowed. His finger went to the collar of my T-shirt.

"This looks cheap, like you work on a farm." His finger moved down from my collar to between my breasts. "Wear something cut lower. Something with buttons."

195

"I don't have that."

"I'll bring something in for you to wear. It's policy."

He took his finger away but managed to drag it over my left breast on its way out. He would be after me every day, all the time, making bigger and bigger demands. I knew I didn't have long before he was telling me that he had to "test" what I would do if a guy wanted a blow job, or wanted to take my shirt off, or wanted me to undress in the back room. I needed a plan.

The good news was that he left before I did; he had me on duty until midnight, and he generally wandered out at around 9:30 or 10:00. The moment his car disappeared I was on the computer, surfing the Internet for jobs, opportunities, anyplace outside Rockland where a person could start with nothing.

There were jobs, sure, but it was understood that the people who applied for these low-paying positions already had homes, food in the pantry, maybe a little money in the bank. What they earned was on top of that.

How did someone get started? I typed "need a job, from a small town" into the search bar. It was an act of frustration; I didn't expect anything to pop up. But the top result was an article from a magazine called *Fem New York* called "The Plight of the Small Town Woman." I started reading it, and my face was wet with tears halfway through. The writer, Faria Grant, might as well have been describing Rockland. She might as well have been profiling Tamara or me or any of the girls I had gone to school with. And the worst part was the last line of her story:

While we would like to believe that America offers endless opportunities for women, some of the girls in these small towns feel as if they've reached a dead end before they are twenty.

196

A Dead End. That was my life.

A father who hated my books. Men in the hardware store who saw me only as an artifact for them to touch. My boss at the motel, hoping to groom me gradually to be his sexual servant.

Some people rang the bell at the main desk. The man, fortyish, a laborer in a flannel shirt, had his arm wrapped tightly around a girl I had gone to high school with. She had been a couple years ahead of me, always laughing and flirting and having fun. She wasn't laughing now. She avoided my eyes as he asked for a room with a vibrating bed. We had five of those, but I said, "Sorry—the beds are currently out of order."

I thought she flashed me a warning look, but it had some gratitude in it.

"That's fucking terrific," he said, squeezing the girl more tightly and glaring at me. "What kind of establishment are you running here?"

"I think you can see what kind," I said, gesturing to the dingy walls.

He leaned in, his chin thrust out. "Are you being a smartass?"

"No, sir. I'm not smart enough to be a smartass."

He didn't like this, but he couldn't think of a comeback, so he handed me his credit card, and I processed his payment. I felt bad for the girl, for all the girls who came in here, but I couldn't make their choices for them.

I gave back his card. "Room Three." I handed him a key. "It has the nicest bathroom," I told her.

She nodded blankly. I touched her arm and whispered, "The bathroom has a good lock."

She nodded again, with the whisper of a smile, and went to join him. As they crossed the lobby toward the door, he swatted her hard on the bottom.

A growling sound came out of my throat. I needed to leave. It didn't matter where I went—just that I broke through that wall. I dialed Tamara on the motel phone. She was probably sitting in the Grill, unless she was with some scummy guy right now.

"Sophia?" She sounded surprised.

"Set it up," I said. "One night, with that trucker who likes missionary position and brunettes. But tell him it will cost two hundred bucks, and it's for one hour."

"What? Okay, I'll see what I can do. How come you changed your mind?"

"Because it's happening anyway. We're all screwed in this town. I just want to get paid for it, so I can never get screwed again."

* * *

I told my dad I had to leave the hardware store early because the motel needed me to help with inventory. It didn't even make sense—they had no inventory. But my dad just shrugged.

"Just make sure he pays you extra. You can buy dinner for me and your mom."

My mom. If I found a way out, I would try to bring her with me. Tamara too. I pictured a sort of Underground Railroad for every Rockland woman who couldn't see beyond her own despair. I would lead them past the quarry and the forest preserve with garbage lining the road, and I would take them to an open field with a rainbow over it.

"The future," I told them in my daydream.

I refused to meet at the Twilight Motel, so I told Tamara that

I'd be at the Loomis Inn, right outside of Rockland. I followed the instructions: to go to the main desk and say I was Mrs. Pitt, and then I should claim the key, go up to the room, and wait.

I was there now, sitting on the edge of the bed, telling myself it was nothing I hadn't done before. Just some guy thrusting into me, pressing his chest into my face, busy with his own fantasies until he finished and went away. I couldn't imagine what we would do for an hour, though, since what he wanted would probably take five minutes.

The door opened, and I looked up to see a man of average height and weight, going gray at the temples. He didn't look crazy or violent, but that didn't guarantee anything. There was risk involved in any random encounter.

You can do this, I told myself. I pictured a Greyhound bus. I pictured that rainbow over a field.

He had been texting when he entered, but now he stopped and looked at me. "You are pretty. Your friend wasn't lying," he said. "Why don't you take that top off?"

You can do this. I had worn a blouse since my pervert boss had made it clear men liked that. I unbuttoned it while he stood there, holding his phone in his hand. I took it off; I had worn no bra, figuring there was no point.

"You have a great body," he said. He stuck his phone in his pocket, walked forward and stood in front of me; first he touched my hair, then my face, then my breasts. I didn't know what to do with my eyes. I stared at his shirt, trying to calm my breathing.

"Relax," he said. "We're going to have fun. Right?" He used one hand to tilt up my face so I would look at him. The other hand was still busy on my chest.

"Right," I said.

"You're not very experienced, huh? What are you, eighteen?"

"Almost nineteen," I said.

"I love it."

"I need to see the money," I said.

He laughed.

"You think I'm going to cheat you?"

"Men do it."

He took out his wallet and showed me how full it was.

"Believe me, I can afford it." He put two hundred dollars on a table by the door. "You can take it when you leave. Now make sure you're worth it."

Something twisted in my stomach; I thought I might throw up.

He was oblivious. He took out his phone again.

"You can take off the rest of your clothes. I just have to finish texting my wife."

My hands froze on the waistband of my pants.

"What do you need to text her about?"

He grinned an annoying grin; it said, *I'm such a naughty boy.*

"I'm telling her that I'm lucky I have her because it's gross how many of the slags at this truck stop are looking for a quick lay."

"Why—why don't you just cheat on her, then? Why go to the trouble of saying she's worth not cheating on?"

"Just covering my bases," he said, his thumbs moving. "Makes me look more authentic."

"But that doubles the offense. Why go through this subterfuge?" I asked, genuinely confused.

He looked up, surprised. Tucking away his phone, he walked over to me and lifted my face so I had to gaze up at him.

"How does a girl like you know a word like that?" he asked.

If he had taken out a two-by-four and banged me in the head with it, it wouldn't have felt like less of an assault than those words. *A girl like me.*

A sudden realization overwhelmed me: for some women, *knowledge* was off limits. And he thought I was one of them.

"Go in the bathroom," I said. "I don't want you to watch me undress."

He squeezed my jaw and considered this, still smiling.

"Okay, little lady. But you do know I'll still see you when I come out?"

"Yeah—I just have a thing about undressing."

"Sure, I can humor my pretty little companion," he said.

He leaned down and kissed me full on the mouth; I almost bit him. I squeezed my eyes shut until it was over, and then I waited until I heard him close the bathroom door. I grabbed my shirt, not bothering to put it on, and went to the door. I tried the knob; thank God, it opened. I flicked his money onto the floor on my way out. Then I ran down the hall and into the stairwell. I didn't figure he'd chase me far. I put my shirt back on and ran down to the exit, then walked the two miles to the Twilight Motel, where my shift was about to start.

Scanlon came wandering over, and I held up a hand.

"I talked to a lawyer, and he said you can't touch me at work. Like, at all. He said to call him if you touch me."

"What?" He tried to look surprised, but I could see that he was incredibly disappointed. "When did I ever touch you?"

"Just be aware," I said.

To my vast relief, he scuttled back into his rathole of an office and didn't come out again until he was ready to leave.

The minute the door closed behind him, I scanned the

parking lot for customers. It was empty and quiet. Then I dove on the computer, clicked onto the Internet, and found the name of the woman who had written the article about small towns. At the end was her email address. I wrote:

Dear Faria Grant: My name is Sophia. My mother said it means wisdom in Greek, but there's no benefit to wisdom in a town like mine, and there's no exit door for a girl who wants to be something other than unhappy. If you can give me any ideas, any insight, about how to get out when I have no money, no one who sympathizes, no one who would applaud for me if I found success, then I would love to hear it. Tonight, in desperation, I almost slept with a man for money. I walked out when he laughed at the idea that I could be intelligent. Please tell me that I'm not one of the girls who will only find a dead end.

I clicked Send before I could change my mind. I got up to handle a reservation for a rumpled-looking salesman, then sat back down and checked my inbox. I checked it a hundred times over the next two hours, and there was nothing. Of course there was nothing. This woman probably got thousands of emails. She didn't know me; I could be some emotionally unstable person or an addict or a murderer. I was a stranger. People didn't help strangers.

At closing time, I moved wearily to the door to flip the sign to Closed. I felt a hundred years old. I wondered how long it took to die once a person realized life wasn't worth living. Could a person die of disappointment? Then I remembered my mother, lying on her bed and staring at the stained ceiling. She had been eighteen once.

I knew that life wasn't only Rockland sterility. I had gone on class trips to beautiful places, where the grass was lush and green and people had bright friendly faces. In my memory, the air was fresher, cooler there, the trees more fragrant. Those other places made me want to keep living, just on the chance that I might return.

I trudged back to the monitor and plopped in my seat to shut it down for the evening. My email said **1 NEW**. I closed my eyes and inhaled. I wanted it to be from her—but in New York, it was one in the morning. She couldn't possibly be checking her email now.

It was an impossible dilemma. I could not click the link. If I did, and it wasn't from her, I would be devastated. If it was from her, and she told me to buzz off or talk to someone in my town like a counselor or clergyperson or that things would get brighter if I hung on, I would destroy Scanlon's office out of sheer rage.

With a scream of frustration, I clicked to my new mail. It was a response from Faria Grant.

I took a deep breath and opened the email.

Hello, Sophia, Faria wrote. *We shouldn't do this via email. Call me now, if you're still awake. Here's my personal number.*

I used the motel phone, waited for three eternal rings.

"Sophia! I'm so glad you called."

* * *

Most people don't know what paradise is, even when they live in it. Paradise is a house so big that you get tired walking from an upstairs bedroom to a downstairs lounge. Paradise is cute little kids who call you "Sotia" and want you to pick them up and cuddle them and tell them silly jokes. Paradise is getting paid to play with those kids and feed them and love them, all of which are easy. It's getting paid in real money and having a beautiful room with a view of a wide green lawn that looks like something out of *The Great Gatsby*. Paradise is having bosses who are grateful for you and keep telling you so—bosses who love each other and kiss each other often and look happy and walk around holding hands. Paradise is Christmastime with this family, sitting on the couch with them like you're a blood relative, drinking eggnog and laughing as the children open presents, and then being handed a pile of presents of your own and an envelope with a card that says Thank You on the front and has five one hundred dollar bills inside. Paradise is when your bosses tell you one day, while you're helping them make dinner, that they don't want to monopolize your time, and that Faria loved the piece you wrote for her magazine, and she thinks she could get you a part-time internship there. Do you think you could do both jobs? And you say, "If I had to work twenty-four hours straight, I would find a way to do both jobs."

If people don't recognize paradise when they see it, they also might not recognize real justice. Justice occurs when you are acknowledged as an individual, thanked for your talents, embraced for your love, and paid for your work. That's social justice. Justice is also served when you tell reporter friends about a small town with a corrupt police force and women forced into servile positions in almost every aspect of life. Those reporters write a story, and investigations begin. Police officers are fired. Men are exposed for soliciting prostitution. The Dry Gulch Grill goes out of business, and the Twilight Motel becomes the focus of several investigations. That's moral justice. Justice occurs when you send your mother a train ticket along with your article "Small Town Phoenix: One Woman's Story" in *Fem New York*. When you tell her that there's an open position for a groundskeeper at a suburban hotel near your community; the person has to have experience with gardening and "a creative vision." They would receive minimum wage and a free basement apartment. And justice is achieved when you meet her at the train in the city; she emerges with one tiny bag and a huge smile, and she looks up at the tall buildings like they are the most beautiful flowers she's ever seen. That's personal justice.

I sent a ticket to Tamara, too, and I told her she only had to be brave enough to make the leap. I told her my employers could find her a nanny job, that their friends were all clamoring for help, and that they would be willing to give her a trial run. She never answered.

Spring came, and I took the children, Pete and Claire, to the ice cream store in their beautiful town, where even the streets looked like someone came and polished them at night. The kids sat eating messily at a checkerboard table that looked like an illustration from *Alice in Wonderland*, and my phone buzzed that I had a text. I thought it might be Faria, asking me if I had emailed some document or where she could find my notes. I never gave myself leisure time without finishing my jobs for Faria. I would have stayed up all night if I needed to, but the wonderful thing about the people in this new world was that they never asked that of me.

I swiped at my phone. Tamara's name appeared.

"Who is it?" asked Claire, her chin dripping chocolate.

"It's a friend of mine."

"Is she coming over?"

I read, "I had no energy left to dream. Thanks for dreaming for me. I'll see you tomorrow." I can define jubilation now, too.

I told Faria a week later that I had a vision in my head. It was like counting sheep at night, except it was women, girls, jumping over a wall and finding life on the other side. Faria said we needed to turn that into a series of articles. She said we could link it with all sorts of resources for women, but also with ways that readers could help. She wanted to feature Tamara, who wasn't a nanny but worked in the coffee bar across from our offices and lived with my mother. She had to commute every day, but she liked the independence. When she got home from her barista job, she helped my mother with shopping, cleaning, and heavy lifting. She was getting strong, she told me, showing me her bicep.

"You are," I agreed, admiring her muscle.

We were all getting strong. We had slung off the rocks of Rockland, the burden of our past, and we were like Atlas set free.

In the summer my employers, Jamie and Phil, threw a party and invited me. They said someone would be there that they would like me to meet. He was tall, with a sweet smile and a bashful air; even I could see that he couldn't stop looking at me. We sat together near the buffet table, and he told me about veterinary school. I told him how much I liked nannying but how much joy I got from working at the magazine. He said he thought I was dynamic.

Later, we talked in their garden, and I said, "I'd like to have dinner with you sometime."

He said, "How about tomorrow?"

"I'll tell you up front," I said, "I don't like people who play games. I don't like subterfuge in a relationship."

"I agree," he said. "You have a terrific vocabulary, by the way. I've been enjoying how clever you are with words."

A fragrant summer breeze rippled the grass and ruffled our hair, making the moment perfect.

* * *

Julia Buckley's short story "Evening Call" won the Sisters in Crime Chicagoland 30th Anniversary Short Story Contest in 2017. Her novel *A Dark and Twisting Path* spent two weeks on the Barnes and Noble mass market bestseller list. Dubbed "a writer to watch" by *Library Journal,* she writes both cozy mysteries and romantic suspense, and she has taught high school English for thirty years. She lives in Chicago with her husband; she has two grown sons and a menagerie of animals. Find out more at www.juliabuckley.com.

The Taste of Collards

by C. C. Guthrie

L izbeth poked at the still firm onion simmering in the pot of black-eyed peas and turned up the flame.

"Peas and collards *again?*"

The scowl on fifteen-year-old Nora's face told Lizbeth what her daughter thought of supper.

"No one's making you eat. If you don't like peas, collard greens, and cornbread, you can march into town and order yourself one of those fancy grilled cheese sandwiches they have at Crawford's lunch counter. I heard they charge a nickel."

Lizbeth would have given anything to serve her son and daughter something different. Nora once said that black-eyed peas tasted like boiled dirt, and cooking greens smelled worse than her brother Billy's feet on a hot summer day. But peas, greens, and cornbread were what they had, so that's what they'd eat.

"If you have five cents, you can add it to our California money," Lizbeth said.

"Do you think Daddy's eating peas, collards, and cornbread out there?" Nora asked.

"Maybe. He's picking berries, but the Knott family must grow other things if they run that chicken restaurant, too. He wrote they're real nice people. They promised us jobs when we get there."

"When can we leave?" Nora asked.

"Still don't have enough money." Lizbeth pumped the well handle, washed her hands, and dried them on the flour sack tucked into the waistband of her skirt that did double duty as an apron and towel. "We'll have to go somewhere else in November when our lease is up. I'm not renewing with Barton." Lizbeth looked at the bare table and frowned. "Nora, do I have to tell you everything? Set the table, and mix up the cornbread. The skillet is right there. Billy will be in soon to eat."

Nora pulled out dishes and silverware for three and asked in a soft voice, "Did you hear about Sissy Post? The girls in school say she went to live with her aunt in Tulsa 'cause Barton did something bad to her. Mae Harper's big sister left last year. She still hasn't come back, and Mae never talks about her."

There'd been talk at church, and the adults had agreed not to tell the children. But rumors were flying again, the way they had about the Harper girl.

"Nora, stay away from Barton. Find an excuse to get away from him. Lie if you have to." Lizbeth saw fear creep into her daughter's eyes. "If he tries to touch you, fight back. Scratch him hard enough to draw blood, so it won't be his word against yours."

"Are you sure you want to give your pretty little girl that advice?"

A large red-faced man stood in the kitchen doorway.

Lizbeth froze, stunned such a big man could enter the house so quietly.

"Alton Barton, you can't walk into this house without an invite. If you want to talk to me, we'll do it on the porch."

"The law says I can inspect my property anytime." He kept his eyes on Nora, who stood with her back to the kitchen pump.

"I'll take Miss Nora to show me around the barn." He opened his jacket to reveal a revolver in a black leather holster.

Lizbeth's stomach heaved.

"Billy can show you around. He's out there now."

"I want Miss Nora to do it." Barton put a beefy hand around the girl's arm. "Deputy Wallace is on his way. When he gets here, send him out to the barn. He'll be real pleased with the inspection we'll be doing."

Lizbeth's blood grew cold at the sight of Barton's evil grin.

Tears streamed down Nora's face as Barton pulled her away from the sink.

"Mama—"

Nora's howl ripped a hole in Lizbeth's heart.

"You stay here and tend to your stinky food and Miss Nora will be back real soon."

Nora cast a desperate look at her mother and tripped. Barton jerked her upright.

The back screen door crashed open and Billy burst in.

"Let her go, Barton!"

The big man yanked Nora around, towering over her.

"Or what? The more trouble you make, the worse it'll be for this one."

Lizbeth grabbed the handle of the cast iron skillet. Barton

swiveled in her direction.

"Nora, move!" Lizbeth shouted.

The girl bent her knees and twisted like she'd seen her brother do in schoolyard scuffles. Barton, thrown off balance, stumbled forward. Lizbeth drew the skillet back and slammed it down on his bowed head. As he swayed, Billy tackled him from behind. They both went down. Barton's head hit the wood floor with a crack.

Barton lay sprawled on the wood floor, his head bent at an unnatural angle.

Billy sat up, a look of surprise on his face. He opened his mouth, but no sound came out.

"Is he dead?" Nora asked.

"Nora, get the hand mirror from my bedroom." She gave Billy the skillet. "Stand behind his head so he can't grab you if he's playing possum. Hit him if he moves."

"Mama, he can't be alive," Billy said. "His neck is as crooked as a dog's leg. It's got to be broken."

Lizbeth knelt beside the still body and took the mirror Nora held out. Her hand shook as she positioned it in front of Barton's mouth. She didn't know what would be worse, if his breath fogged the glass or if it didn't. The mirror stayed clear.

"Mama, you gave him a good wallop," Billy said. "Why isn't there more blood?"

"Dead men don't bleed," Lizbeth said. "Enough talk. Was Barton's wagon out back when you came in?"

Billy slowly shook his head.

"Run. Go find it," she said. "Don't dither. We have to hide Barton. He said Deputy Wallace is on his way here." Lizbeth focused on what else had to be done now that she was sure the man was dead. "Nora, mix up the cornbread. Wash the skillet before you pour in the batter."

Hinges shrieked and the back door slammed.

"Mama, his horse and wagon are in the barn," Billy said.

"Bring the wagon up here and park it by the steps," Lizbeth said. "While you do that, Nora and I will move Barton to the back door."

"How are we going to do that?" Nora asked. "He's awful big."

"I'll show you. Quick, take the top sheet off my bed and put the coverlet back on while I finish up here."

Lizbeth struggled to maneuver Barton's holster around his belly to remove the revolver. The bullets went into her apron pocket along with his wallet after she stuffed the bills into her blouse. She was checking the simmering peas and greens when Nora returned with the sheet.

"Spread it on the floor beside him," Lizbeth said. "Remember how we made up the bed for Granny when she was too sick for us to move? We roll him one way, tuck the sheet under him, roll him the other way, and pull the sheet straight so we can drag him."

When the body and the wagon were in position, Lizbeth eyed the distance between the back steps and the wagon. The horse hitched to the front neighed softly and nuzzled the dirt. She took that as agreement her plan would work.

"We've only got to get him down to the second step to shift him onto the wagon," she said. "Nora, take hold of the sheet by his feet. Billy, grab that edge by his head, and I'll take this one. We'll go out first and pull until he starts to slide."

By the time they had Barton loaded on the wagon, they were panting and sweating, but Lizbeth pushed them to move faster.

"Billy, take the wagon up the back lane to Uncle Major's old place. From the clearing behind the house, you can see the county road in both directions. Make sure no one's heading to the bridge."

"What if someone is there?" Nora asked.

"Won't be," Billy said. "No one's been up there since Uncle Major left for California, and no one will be until they sell it for taxes."

"Wish we were in California now," Nora whispered.

"Hush, now," Lizbeth said. "Run get Billy the paring knife from the kitchen." She gestured for Billy to climb on the wagon. "When you get to Major's, cut the stitches on the bridle. If the road is clear, cross the bridge, and turn the wagon around so it looks like he was heading this way."

Nora handed Billy the knife.

"Pull the bridle apart, let the horse go, then unhook the hitch. Push the wagon down the hill beside the bridge." Lizbeth looked off in the distance, imagining how it might happen. "Folks need to think something made the horse bolt. Better get go—oh, here." She handed over Barton's wallet. "Put this in his jacket," she said. "We need folks to think he was robbed after the wagon ran off the road. When you're done, run straight back. If anyone sees you, say you've been checking the garden. It can't be seen from here or the road, so no one can say any different. Now go. You can do this." She added a silent prayer as her son drove off.

"Nora, run out to the barn and scuff away any wagon wheel marks." She kicked at the dirt to show her daughter what to do. "I'll check out front."

For once, the drought worked in their favor. There was no sign of recent car or wagon traffic on the county road or in front of the house. Lizbeth fingered the bullets in her pocket as she crossed the hard-packed dirt road to a sagging barbed wire fence on the other side. She wouldn't allow any more deaths. One was bad enough. She sprinkled the bullets in the weeds along the fence line.

Back in the kitchen, she urged her daughter to hurry.

"Nora, wash your face and finish up the cornbread, so we can eat when Billy gets back," Lizbeth said. When the skillet went into the oven, she closed her eyes, took a deep breath, and pressed her right hand against the collard pot.

Lizbeth screamed and jerked away from the stove.

"Water, Nora. Quick. I burned my hand." Anguish crossed her face, and Nora began to cry. The girl's tears fell as fast as she pumped the well handle.

Lizbeth thrust her hand under the spout and watched her palm turn red and blister. Finally, she put her good hand on top of Nora's.

"That's enough water. Get the salve and a cloth to wrap up my hand before Wallace gets here."

Nora had stopped crying, although her face was still red and swollen, when she tied the last knot on Lizbeth's bandage. At the sound of a car out front, she grew anxious again.

A heavy hand banged on the flimsy screen door. A uniformed sheriff's deputy stood on the porch.

"I'm looking for Alton Barton," he said.

Lizbeth waited for him to show common courtesy and remove his hat.

"Ma'am? Have you seen Barton?"

Lizbeth pushed open the door.

He walked in, his hat still on his head, his revolver in a black leather holster on his hip. He sniffed and looked around the room.

"Barton isn't here," Lizbeth said.

Wallace looked from Nora's tear-stained face to Lizbeth's bandaged hand.

"What happened to you?"

"Burned my hand on a pot of collards."

"Is that what that smell is? Glad I've never had them."

Lizbeth shrugged.

"No point in asking you to stay for supper. If I see Barton, I'll tell him you're looking for him."

The back door banged.

"Mama, I'm starving," Billy yelled. "When are we going to—" At the sight of Wallace, he stopped short. "What's going on—Mama, your hand! What happened?"

"Burned it," Lizbeth said. "Have you seen Barton today? Deputy Wallace is looking for him."

"Only old man Post passed by this morning when I was in the pasture. I just came from the garden." He beamed. "The tomatoes, lettuce, and carrots are about ready to sell. But we won't have many watermelons. Those damn coyotes bit chunks out of half our crop."

"Billy, I've told you not to use that word in this house. Deputy, I need to feed my family so I can lie down. My hand is hurting, and I feel woozy."

"Your husband went to California, didn't he? 'Bout six months ago?"

Lizbeth's response was a silent stare. He knew when her husband left to find work, and she wouldn't give him the satisfaction of confirming it.

"Why would Barton tell me he was coming here and not show up?" Wallace asked.

"Don't know," Lizbeth said. "You'll have to ask him."

Before he could respond, an old truck careened off the road

and jerked to a halt next to the deputy's car. Steam shot from beneath the hood. The engine sputtered and backfired twice. The driver's door flew open and a barefoot young man wearing tattered overalls, a faded shirt, and a frayed straw hat bolted out.

As he leaped to the porch, he shouted, "Deputy Wallace! Wagon down in the Jim Fork, on the north side."

Wallace opened the screen door.

"Anyone hurt?"

The boy removed his hat as he entered the house.

"Ma'am," he said courteously. Only then did he answer Wallace. "I didn't see anyone, Deputy. Old man Post sent me to fetch you from town and he went to look for a body in the water. Lucky I saw your car here."

"Billy, go with them and help," Lizbeth said.

Her son stared at her.

"Mama!"

"I know, you want your supper," Lizbeth said. "But if we don't lend a hand, folks won't be there for us when we need help. Nora, get Billy some cornbread to eat on the way."

The barefoot driver watched as Billy took the cornbread from Nora.

"I'll drive you to the bridge and back here if you give me a bite of that."

Lizbeth took in the too-short overalls and bare feet.

"Nora, get him a piece, too." She peered at the boy. "What's your name? I don't know you."

"Garvis Harper, Ma'am."

"Harper, did you see the wagon go into the water?" Wallace asked.

"No, just the marks it made going down the hill."

Wallace crossed his arms.

"Don't you live on the south side of town? Why are you over this way?"

Garvis looked at Lizbeth.

"I took my mama to Spiro early this morning to stay with my aunt," he said. "Mama's been poorly this year, and I thought a visit with her sister might perk her up."

Wallace scowled.

"On the way back, when I got to the bridge, that's when I saw the wheel tracks in the grass."

Nora returned with Garvis' cornbread.

"Are you Mae Harper's brother?" she asked, handing him the slice.

He nodded and took a bite. A look of contentment flooded his face.

Wallace left the youngsters talking and surveyed the kitchen, the table set for three, the skillet of cornbread with two generous wedges missing, and two simmering pots. Steam swirled up when he lifted the lid on the peas. It slipped from his fingers and fell back on the pot with a clang. His hand moved to the lid on the greens.

"Sure you don't want some peas and collards before you go?" Lizbeth asked.

Wallace turned away from the stove.

"My wife promised me chicken and dumplings tonight," he said as he walked by. "Boys, need to get to the bridge." He gave one last look around before he followed Billy and Garvis out the door.

* * *

217

Later that night, Billy woke Lizbeth dozing on the sofa.

"Mama, Barton's gone. He wasn't in the wagon or in the water. Not in the mud, not along the edge, and there isn't enough water in the Jim Fork for him to float away. He's just gone."

Lizbeth saw her son tremble from exhaustion and hunger and fixed him a bowl of peas, greens, and cornbread.

After he finished eating, he asked, "What could have happened to Barton?"

"I don't know," she said. "He was dead when you rode off with his body."

Billy flinched.

"Tell me what happened at the bridge."

"I did everything you said. He was in the wagon when it rolled it down the hill. I saw him."

Lizbeth closed her eyes and rubbed her forehead.

"Get to bed. We'll talk about it tomorrow."

When she was alone, she retrieved Barton's revolver, dried it off, and cleaned the kitchen for the second time that night.

* * *

The next morning, Lizbeth gathered the eggs after Billy left for the pasture and Nora for school. She shooed the birds into the yard to peck for worms and pushed aside the straw under the roost of the meanest hen in the flock.

She added the bills from Barton's wallet to their California money in the Mason jar under a rock. His revolver went into the hole under the next roost. After the straw was back in place, she left the hen house with the eggs and met Garvis as he rounded the corner of the house. He was still barefoot, wearing patched overalls that barely skimmed his ankles, a clean shirt, and his battered hat. She heard his idling truck cough and sputter in the distance.

He whipped off his hat.

"Ma'am," Garvis said. "Thank you for your kindness yesterday. Your cornbread was the best I've tasted in a long time. My mama used to make it but she doesn't cook much since my sister died."

"Mae? She died?"

He shook his head.

"Mae is my little sister. Our big sister died last year."

"I'm sorry. I didn't know that."

"Mama told us not to talk about it." He clutched his hat between his hands and looked down at his bare feet as if making a decision. "Billy doesn't need to worry. No one will ever know what happened yesterday."

Lizbeth's heart thumped so hard she was sure he could hear it.

"Me and old man Post made sure no one will ever find Barton. He'll never hurt anyone again. When I saw him in the wagon rolling into the Jim Fork, I 'bout cheered."

Lizbeth chose her words carefully.

"You saw the wagon go into the water?"

He nodded.

"I was squirrel hunting in the woods beside the bridge. I'd parked past the bend, so Billy didn't see my truck. Usually I don't turn it off." He flashed a quick grin. "I can't always get it started again, but I thought I'd be hunting for a while, so I took a chance."

* * *

That night Lizbeth didn't serve collards. The family sat down to a supper of black-eyed peas, cornbread, and fresh-picked lettuce with vinegar and hot bacon drippings. Her children's joy was worth the missed sale.

"Mama, I'm glad we're not having greens tonight. The ones last night didn't taste right," Billy said.

"Really?"

She'd noticed the unpleasant metallic taste, too. Next time she cooked collards, she'd use her original recipe and leave out the revolver.

* * *

C. C. Guthrie's short stories have appeared in the anthologies *Fish Out of Water, Busted! Arresting Stories From The Beat, Fishy Business,* and *Landfall: The Best New England Crime Stories 2018.* She lives near Fort Worth, Texas.

Chrissie

by Carole Sojka

C hrissie spent a long time dressing for her trip. She blow-dried her hair until its volume nearly overwhelmed her small face, then put on the new skirt and top she and her mother had bought. The skirt was too long, but after she turned the waistband over twice under the dark blue knitted top, it was just the right length. Although she wore the new training bra they'd bought, she still didn't fill out the top.

In the mirror, she looked very grown up. She wasn't allowed to wear makeup, but she rubbed a little lipstick on her cheeks for color. She'd gotten the lipstick with some of the money Grandma had sent for her birthday, although she'd told her mother she'd spent it all on the pretty silver bracelet. She stashed the tube in her bag. She could put it on after she got rid of her mother.

Mom looked critically at the new skirt when she came downstairs.

"Isn't it awfully short?" she asked. "I didn't remember that it was so short. I don't think you should wear something that short."

"You said it was okay when we bought it." Chrissie worked on sounding slightly injured at her mother's change of mind.

Still fussing about the skirt, her mother drove her to the airport and hovered, anxious.

"Are you sure you'll be all right? Shall I get you something to drink on the plane?"

"Don't fuss, Mom. I'll be fine."

When at last it was time to board, Chrissie kissed her mother and hid herself in among the people waiting to get through the gate. Out of the corner of her eye, she tried not to see her mother standing on tiptoe, peering over the heads of the people on line, looking for Chrissie's red hair. Chrissie ducked and sneaked further along.

"Don't let her call me," she prayed. "Just let me get through the gate without her seeing me."

Clutching her boarding pass, she hurried up to the gate entrance farthest away from her mother, trying to stay behind the bulk of the man beside her so that her mother couldn't see her standing by herself. It didn't work.

"Chrissie! Do your summer reading. And remember! Don't talk to strangers."

Omigod, would she never stop?

Finally Chrissie was on the plane. The flight attendant looked at her boarding pass, then at Chrissie.

"Flying alone?" she asked.

"Yes," Chrissie said and hurried down the aisle, her carry-on bag bumping her legs and careening into the seats on either side.

"Someday," Chrissie said to herself as she looked enviously at the passengers in first class already relaxing with their drinks, their seats reclined, their legs outstretched. "Someday. I swear it."

She found her seat, the window she'd asked her mother to request, and standing on tiptoes, she hoisted her bag overhead into the bin.

"Excuse me," she said to the man seated on the aisle. "I'm at the window."

He stepped into the aisle to let her through. He wore a cowboy hat, which he took off when he got up, although she thought he was too old to be a cowboy. The middle seat was empty, and with luck, it would stay that way.

She took out her small mirror and carefully applied her lipstick. She made a kiss on a tissue to blot her lips, then checked her hair. She thought she looked pretty good, but when she was grown up, she swore she'd always fly first class, and all her makeup would be really expensive, like Chanel or L'Oréal.

The summer evening was dark, and staring out the window, she couldn't see much except scattered airport lights. The flight was a red-eye, crossing the country overnight and getting her into Tampa at seven in the morning by her grandparents' clock. It was the only non-stop flight there was. Her mother insisted that if Chrissie wanted to fly alone she couldn't change planes in Memphis or Atlanta.

"That's too dangerous," her mother had said. "You're too young."

She had protested, but eventually she had consented to take the red-eye, as long as her mother promised not to tell the airline that she was only eleven or that she was traveling alone. She didn't want anyone to make a fuss over her. After all, she was pretty grown up now. She thought she looked at least fifteen. She didn't need a flight attendant to babysit her.

Uh-oh, the middle seat was not going to stay empty. Here was a man, a businessman from the look of him, who said, "Excuse me, I think I'm on the aisle."

The man who had earlier claimed the aisle seat moved over and sat next to Chrissie. He looked old to Chrissie, at least as old as her father. He wore jeans and a sports shirt, not a suit like the man now seated on the aisle, and he held the cowboy hat on his lap. When he tried to stow it overhead, the flight attendant asked him to hold it or put it under his seat.

He smiled at Chrissie. "Sorry about this," he said. "I thought the middle would stay empty, but I guess it's a full flight."

"I guess so," she said.

After the tiny bag of peanuts and a glass of orange juice, the flight attendant gave her a blanket. Chrissie spread it over her legs, concealing the new skirt now hiked high up on her thighs. The blanket warmed her legs and feet, chilly now with the air conditioning blasting. The plane climbed and traveled high over New Mexico and Colorado. Her eyes closed. She thought about what she would do in Florida with her grandparents—Disney World, of course, and Sea World and the Gulf beaches. She wondered if that cute boy who had been there last year—Justin was his name—would be visiting his grandparents again this year.

She woke to the throbbing of engines and the presence of something odd and heavy in her lap. It took her a moment to remember where she was. But what was on her lap, under the blanket? She touched it gingerly. It wasn't hard, like a book, and it kind of indented under the pressure of her fingers. What was it? She reached under the blanket and touched the odd, heavy thing. It felt warm and fleshy, like a hand.

Was it her hand that had fallen asleep? Both her hands seemed awake. She pinched the thing carefully, but she felt nothing. It wasn't hers. It must be the hand of the man next to her. She turned to look at him, but he didn't appear to notice her look or feel her touch.

The plane was dark. Could she be mistaken? Was this a hand or something else entirely? Perhaps he didn't realize he'd put his hand in her lap.

What should she say? "Excuse me, sir. I think your hand is in my lap."

It couldn't be his hand. He would have noticed. She wriggled and tried to push it away, but it was heavy, and it just stayed there. It didn't move. She stole another glance at the man. He appeared to be asleep, his eyes closed, his head slumped to one side, and his face turned away. The man on the aisle was still awake, the overhead light shining on his laptop while he concentrated on his work. He wasn't paying any attention to Chrissie or to the man next to her.

Well, she'd just pick up the hand and return it to its owner. If she were careful, maybe he wouldn't even wake up.

Cautiously, she peeled back the blanket and picked up the hand—it was a hand, she could see in the dim light—and put it on the lap of the man next to her. His face was still averted. He didn't stir.

Satisfied, she looked at her watch. One o'clock. She'd only slept for an hour. Still more than three hours to go. Nothing to see out the window. Just darkness. She closed her eyes and dozed.

She dreamed. There was something touching her, something touching her leg, something warm and heavy. She jerked awake, then realized the hand was back. The hand was moving slowly, carefully, the fingers gently touching the warm flesh under her skirt.

She looked at the man next to her. It was his hand, wasn't it? Should she say something? What could she say? Perhaps she could tell one of the flight attendants. But the plane was dark and quiet, and she couldn't see any of the flight attendants around.

Should she yell at the man? "Get your hand off my leg?" She couldn't stand the thought of the commotion that would cause. People making a fuss. The man denying everything.Everyone looking at her as though she was crazy.

Then, what would the flight attendants do? Would they believe her? Where else could she sit? The flight was full. Maybe they would just leave her there, still sitting next to him.

She couldn't finish out the flight with everyone looking at her, saying, "She's too young to be traveling alone. Look at her. Look at what's happened. What was her mother thinking?"Then someone would tell her grandparents, and they would tell her mother, and she'd never ever be able to travel alone again.

Just leave it alone. What could he do on a plane full of people? It wasn't unpleasant, really. Just sort of odd. The warm fingers on the soft part of her leg, inside her thigh, caressing, caressing. It was even kind of nice. There was a warm tingly feeling between her legs, a pleasant feeling, exciting. It was the feeling she got when she touched herself, but of course she wouldn't do that on the plane. But that was what the man was doing. His hand was reaching inside her leg.

She glanced over at him, but he still had his eyes closed and his face turned away from her. The hand, which didn't seem to belong to him, moved slowly, gently, inside her thigh, up between her legs.

Then she felt it. A finger. Inside her panties. Just a finger, but she nearly jumped out of her skin. He was touching her. She could feel herself flush, grow warm, as he moved his finger around on the soft moist flesh between her legs, gently touching, caressing. This couldn't be happening to her. But it was.

She was wet between her legs. She could feel the wetness and the tingle. She knew he could feel it too. She turned to look out the window. Beyond the lights on the wing, she could see only darkness. What should she do? She couldn't scream now. It was too late. It had gone too far. She should have done something before. Now she couldn't fling the hand away.

Just let him do it, she thought. Just let him. It's not that much further to Tampa. I can't stop him now. What would I say? He'd say I'm crazy or imagining things. It doesn't feel so bad.

* * *

The flight attendant served the passengers coffee and a stale sweet roll before they began their descent into Tampa. She didn't look at the man while they ate or after they landed and taxied toward the gate. Once they could stand, he busied himself with retrieving his luggage from the overhead bin.

"Can I get your bag down, young lady?" he asked. The "young lady" really galled her. After what he'd been doing!

"It's checked," she said.

Chrissie sat in her window seat while most of the passengers hurried off the plane. Then she took her turn when someone let her into the aisle, retrieved her carry-on, and followed the crowd through coach and into first class. She stepped aside at the exit and turned toward the flight attendant who was standing there.

"I don't really know whether I should say something," she said softly. "But the man who sat next to me had a knife in his suitcase."

"Are you sure?" the flight attendant said. She wore a badge that said *Heidi*.

"I'm pretty sure I saw it when he opened his suitcase," Chrissie said. "Before he put it in the luggage thing, he opened it and got something out. I knew it was dangerous 'cause my uncle has one just like that. It doesn't look real scary, but it's sharp."

"Is he still on the plane?" Heidi asked.

"No. He got off ahead of me, but he's wearing a cowboy hat. He had it on his lap the whole time we were flying because there wasn't any room with the luggage."

"Wait here a minute, hon," Heidi said. She turned and went into the cockpit. When Chrissie turned and left, she saw the flight attendant talking to the pilot.

Her Nana and Grandpa were waiting at the luggage carousel where the bags from her flight were circling. The plane had been early, just a bit, and they were happy to see her. They hugged her, first Nana, then Grandpa, then Nana again.

"We're so glad you're here," Nana said.

"There's my bag," Chrissie said, and Grandpa grabbed the suitcase off the carousel.

When she glanced around, she was pleased to see the man in the cowboy hat being led away by two airport policemen. From what Chrissie could see, he was complaining loudly, but the policemen were hurrying him along, ignoring his protests.

Chrissie decided she'd for sure wear jeans on the flight home.

* * *

Carole Sojka is the author of three mystery novels: two set on Florida's Treasure Coast and a standalone, *Psychic Damage*, set in Southern California. She has had short stories published in an anthology from Red Coyote Press, *The Storyteller*, *Yellow Mama*, and other venues. The most exciting time of Carole's life were the two years she spent teaching in Africa with the Peace Corps at a time of great hope for the newly independent countries of Africa. Upon her return, her Master's degree in Public Administration enabled her to work as the administrator in a public law office. She lives in Southern California with her husband and two spoiled dogs.

Discussion Questions

The Anthology as A Whole

1. What did you learn that you didn't know before? What surprised you? Moved you? Made you angry? Made you laugh?

2. Was there anything in the stories that you don't believe could happen in real life? What, and why not?

3. Besides being crime fiction writers, some of the authors in this anthology are a therapist, a police officer, a lawyer, a scientist, a historian, and a high school teacher. How do you think these professions might cause their perspectives on crimes against women and girls to differ?

4. What do you think of the editor's decision to include only women authors? What might have been different if men had written some of the stories?

5. Which was your favorite story? Why? Was there a story that you particularly disliked or found uncomfortable to read or think about? Why?

"Never Again" by Elizabeth Zelvin

1. "Child sexual abuse is far more prevalent than most people realize." "About 1 in 10 children will be abused before their

18th birthday." (1 in 7 girls, 1 in 25 boys) "60% of child abuse victims never tell anyone." "Of children who are sexually abused, 20% are abused before the age of 8." These eye-opening statistics come from a 2017 online fact sheet by an organization called Darkness to Light at http://www.d2l.org. Does this information surprise you? Does it change your beliefs in any way?

2. Did reading this story in Valerie's and Frances's points of view help you understand what it might be like to live through such experiences? How does reading a short story compare with reading facts and statistics as a way to comprehend a complex social issue such as child molestation? Do you think crime fiction publishers and magazines should ban stories about child abuse?

3. What do you think of the attitudes of Valerie's and Frances's mothers and those of the other adults in the story: Valerie's aunt, the sex education teacher, the members of Frances's church?

4. What is your attitude toward fat? Is weight important to you for yourself? For the people you know? Do you routinely judge people by their body size? Do you think obesity should be considered an issue that calls for sensitivity, like race, gender, and sexual orientation?

5. Do you understand Frances's statement about feeling simultaneously invisible and conspicuous? Have you ever felt either or both? What caused you to feel that way? If it happened now, could you do anything to change it?

"Pentecost" by Eve Fisher

1. What are some of the difficulties Darla faces in being the first female pastor in rural South Dakota?

2. When Darla was a child, she decided not tell her parents what Roger Olson did to her. Do you think she should have told? Why?

3. Why do you think Roger Olson's mother looked "defiant" when child Darla returned from the back room after her childhood encounter with Roger?

4. Portia Davison, Darla Koenig, Mary Lenvik, and Emmie Norred all have different roles in Laskin society, from "trailer trash" to an elderly pillar of the church. Is there anything that links them? How have their relationships with men in the community affected them?

5. What do you think would have been the best way to deal with Roger Olson's continuing behavior as a peeping Tom who also exposes himself to young girls?

"The Call Is Yours" by Rona Bell

1. What are your feelings about what happens to the narrator? To what extent do you feel empathy? judgment? ambivalence? What else?

2. What do you think the author is saying about memory in this story?

3. What impact do you think the passage of time has for the narrator? In this story, to what extent do you think time heals or causes pain to fester? In general?

4. What do you think of the role of the police in the events of this story? Do you think they do enough? Do you think the detective said the right thing to the narrator? If not, what might she have said?

5. Do you think a campaign such as "The Call Is Yours" is effective in righting wrongs and changing attitudes toward women?

"The Final Recall" by Diana Catt

1. "The Final Recall" is layered with ethical dilemmas. What are they, and how does Sara deal with them? What do you think of her decisions? Are there other choices she could have made?

2. Do you agree with Sara that her primary investigator and boss, Dr. Kolb, undervalues her degree? If so, would you consider this a form of sexual harassment? Why, or why not?

3. Why do you think Dr. Kolb murders Monique? Was the ending a satisfying form of justice for you as a reader?

4. If the near-future premise of this story became reality, how would you feel about having your memories digitized as videos after your death?

"A Measured Death" by Julia Pomeroy

1. Do you believe a woman like Mary might respond to a man like Jan differently today in the same circumstances, or might she make the same choices, at age eighteen and later?

2. To what extent do you think Jan's behavior is justified by the drive and focus he uses to produce his level of achievement and artistry? What do you think of one or more people being sacrificed in the service of genius?

3. How important to the story is it that Mary has no friends or family around her? Where do you think this is most clearly illustrated? Do you believe people must have a support system in order to break free of an abusive situation?

4. What do you feel toward Mary? Do you have sympathy for her? Do you think she should have made different choices, stood up for herself better, or tried harder to get out? What other options do you think she had?

5. Do you believe you could ever find yourself in Mary's

situation? What factors might have put you there? Love? Economic dependence? Physical intimidation? Being awed by someone's great gift, as Mary is by Jan's?If so, what would you do about it?

"Miss Evelyn Nesbit Presents" by Ana Brazil

1. During her luncheon with producer H. H. Samson, Evelyn attempts to take back the story of her life. Does she succeed? If so, do you think that she could continue to own her life? If not, what else could she have done?

2. Do you think Evelyn's actions in the hotel dining room would have been different if she hadn't listened to the conversation in the train car? What might have happened?

3. The author of this story deliberately kept the lush and sensual details of 1914 to a minimum so as not to romanticize the era and to keep the focus on Evelyn's resolution. Did you miss those visual details? Or, knowing that the story was set in 1914, did you still see Evelyn outfitted like Rose in *Titanic* or Lady Mary in *Downton Abbey*? In short stories, how important is how we envision historical characters versus the actions that they take?

4. Is H. H. Samson redeemable? In 1914, could a man like him ever learn to treat women with respect? To what extent do men like H.H. still operate today? Does society still condone them to the same extent?

5. When Evelyn was a young teenager, her beauty was celebrated by numerous photographers and painters. She was even Charles Dana Gibson's inspiration for his famous Gibson Girl. Did Evelyn's beauty and occupations as a model and chorus girl doom her to be a Me oo victim and survivor? How would these occupations have served her in the 21st century?

"Stepping on Snakes" by Madeline McEwen

1. "Stepping on Snakes" is set in South Africa in the early 1960s. What elements of the setting coincided with what you already knew about South Africa during that era? What elements surprised you?

2. The author chose not to focus on apartheid and the status of the black and so-called colored people of South Africa, which is what most Americans associate most readily with South Africa. Why do you think she might have done this? How do you feel about her choice to focus on other aspects of South African life?

3. Bobbie is seven years old. Were you aware of this as you read the story? Did you find Bobbie's characterization convincing, given her stated age? If not, what age do you think the author might have made her more effectively?

4. The naive and well-behaved Celeste is a foil for Bobbie. Did you find the use of this device satisfying in "Stepping on Snakes"? In general, do you think it is an effective way to develop character and conflict in a story? How else might the author have shown Bobbie's independence and curiosity?

5. In the climactic scene in the story, a man outside the schoolyard fence exposes himself to Bobbie and her classmates. What elements of this scene could have happened in any time and place? Which do you think were particular to that era and setting? What do you think of the reaction of Bobbie's teacher? Why do you think Bobbie never told anyone what happened?

"Women Who Love Dogs" by Dayle A. Dermatis

1. John believes women should find him attractive and want to date him without knowing anything about him. His attitude

is shared by "incels" and some other men. What do you think of the idea that men "deserve" women and/or sex or that women have a duty to perform for men?

2. Vanessa cares for her sister, Brooke, who has MS. Some male doctors are reported to discount or disbelieve women's pain and other symptoms. Have you or a loved one had such an experience? How do you think the medical community might be educated differently?

3. Officer Ortiz believes Vanessa's and Brooke's story. Have you had an experience where a police officer discounted your report because of gender or another form of bias? How did that make you feel? Are there ways to educate police on how to listen to women and others who may be stereotyped and disregarded?

4. Rent-A-Pup is fictional, but the sharing economy is real. Lyft, Uber, AirBnB, and Poshmark allow individuals to share goods and services without accessing traditional corporate models. How do these services affect women in particular both positively and negatively?

"Jewel's Hell" by Lynn Hesse

1. "Jewel's Hell" is set in the projects in Atlanta, Georgia. To what extent do you think the prevalence and patterns of domestic abuse differ in impoverished and prosperous environments?

2. How do you feel about reading a story in which the main villain is a woman in an anthology of Me Too stories? What or whom do you tend to blame for societal patterns of violence, disrespect for women, and similar social ills? In light of your beliefs, does this story make you uncomfortable?

3. Bess is cruel and abusive toward her daughters, but she

herself was molested by her father as a child. Does that fact make you feel any sympathy for her?

4. How do you imagine Jewel's frame of mind as she walks down the hallway with a gun to face Bess? What is your opinion of her mental health, her sense of responsibility, her justification for what we know she is about to do? Do you think the presence of a gun in the home contributes to the probability of violence or offers protection?

5. What do you think of Jewel's decision not to leave because she won't leave Callie behind, and then, when Callie escapes, to take drastic measures to make sure her sister stays free? Is it a sacrifice? An act of love? Foolish and unnecessary? What other options might she have had?

"Banshee Scream" by Gin Gannon

1. Traditionally, banshees—unlike the protagonist of "Banshee Scream"—are powerless female creatures, unable to do more than weep and wail. Can you think of other passive females in mythology and folklore? Suppose you re-imagined one of them as taking back her power while retaining elements of her traditional character? Which one would you choose? How would you empower her?

2. The banshee in this story is only called out when a killer is likely to evade justice. Do you believe this killer would have gone free if not for the banshee's intervention? How often do you think doctors get away with murder? Do you think any group is unfairly protected from accountability toward the law? If so, what groups or categories of people?

3. The killer in "Banshee Scream" is in a special position of power in relation to the victim. To what extent do you think women face a greater disparity in power than men in doctor-

patient relationships? In what other power-based situations do you think women may be mistreated more often than men or suffer more significant consequences?

4. The banshee isn't allowed to carry out the punishment until the killer confesses. Why do you think that rule exists? How does it serve the killer to admit his guilt out loud? Why or how is it important to the banshee to hear that admission on behalf of his victim?

5. Women are often labeled "crazy," as the banshee is by the killer, when they say or do things that men don't like. Has that ever happened to you or anyone you know?

"No Outlet" by V.S. Kemanis

1. Do you think Arlene's feelings of guilt at age 64 about the crime against her college roommate are justified or an overreaction? How does Arlene's past shape her behavior toward her new neighbor Cherise? In what ways is Arlene different than she was 45 years ago?

2. It looks to Arlene as if Cherise is "hiding away." Do you think Cherise is strong or weak? How easy or difficult is it for a woman to run away and hide from an abuser? Has Cherise dealt with her situation in an effective way for herself? For her son?

3. Arlene is motivated to help Cherise in any way she can. Is Arlene a Good Samaritan or just a nosy neighbor? Should women look out for each other? If you found yourself in this situation, would you try to help or look the other way?

4. Have you ever been involved in a relationship with someone who stalked you or wouldn't take No for an answer? How did you deal with it? What are some possible ways to deal with someone who feels entitled? To what extent do men as well as women ever experience this kind of harassment?

"A Dog's Life" by Ann Rawson

1. "A Dog's Life" is set in Liverpool in the UK in 1980. Do you think attitudes to rape in the UK and/or the US have changed since then?

2. Liz decides against reporting her attacker to either to the college authorities or the police. Why do you think victims find it hard to report being attacked? Do you think it's easier now than it was back in 1980?

3. Dominic, who attempts to rape Liz, is an attractive middle class boy from a good family. Is there a difference in how accused rapists are perceived depending on race or class? Has that changed over time?

4. The term "date rape" originated in the mid-1970s but didn't become widely used until the late 1980s. The great majority of rape victims know their attackers. In the UK, some rape cases have been dropped by the prosecution service because of messaging that could be interpreted as exonerating the accused. How do you think changes in technology have affected the issue of consent and whether the victim's story is convincing to investigators and juries?

5. In the story, Liz fights back. In reality, victims often freeze or comply out of fear for their lives. What difference do you think that makes to how victims feel and how they are treated by the justice system? Is there still a sense that there are "good victims" and "bad victims"? What other factors make a difference to whether victims are believed or not?

"Subterfuge" by Julia Buckley

1. Sofia sees herself as an agent for change. Do you think she is exceptional or that there are many Sofias in small towns? Do you think that her mother or her friend really needed her

help, or would they have found their own way out eventually?

2. What do you think of the concept of patriarchy as a way of explaining the social realities of Rockland?

3. Do you think that any of the men in the story are helping Sofia? What do you think the motivations for their behavior are, conscious and unconscious?

4. What is your reaction to Sofia considering prostitution as a possible way out? Would you feel differently if Sofia used sex to get what she wanted without asking direct payment for it?

5. What do you think of the ending of "Subterfuge?" Does it seem realistic or even possible to you? If not, are you able to accept it as a fable or parable? If you are dissatisfied with or skeptical about the ending, how would you have ended it?

"The Taste of Collards" by C.C. Guthrie

1. As a rural landlord in the 1930s, Barton seems to have almost infinite power over his tenants. How different do you think that is today? What resources would tenants like Lizbeth have that she wouldn't have had at the time?

2. "The Taste of Collards" paints a vivid picture of poverty in the country. What elements of that poverty made an impression on you? How might poverty in the city differ from the conditions in which Lizbeth and her family live?

3. What do you think of the way Lizbeth dealt with the threat to her daughter, both before and after Barton's arrival? What other options might she have had?

4. The author uses Deputy Wallace's refusal to take off his hat as a symbol of his lack of respect for Lizbeth. How important does this seem to you? Is respect as represented by good manners important in the culture you grew up in? In

your grandparents' culture?

5. Did you create a picture of Lizbeth and her son and daughter in your mind as you read the story? Did you assign a race to them or wonder whether they were black or white? How important do you think race would have been in the culture of rural poverty in the 1930s? Today?

"Chrissie" by Carole Sojka

1. Chrissie takes a cross-country night flight by herself to visit her grandparents. What do you think of an eleven-year-old girl traveling alone overnight? Would you feel differently in the case of a boy?

2. What do you think motivates Chrissie's seat-mate's behavior? Do you think it is planned or opportunistic? To what extent do you think it is motivated by Chrissie's youth? By the fact that she is trying to look older?

3. What options does Chrissie have other than letting the man do what he does? How do you think she might have treated him if she had been fifteen? Seventeen?

4. What do you think of what Chrissie does to punish her abuser? What else might she have done?

About the Editor

Elizabeth Zelvin, editor, previously edited the anthology *Where Crime Never Sleeps: Murder New York Style 4.* Her stories have appeared in *Ellery Queen's Mystery Magazine* and *Alfred Hitchcock's Mystery Magazine* and have been nominated three times each for the Derringer and Agatha awards for Best Short Story. She is the author of the Bruce Kohler Mysteries and the

Mendoza Family Saga, a series of Jewish historical novels and mystery short stories. In addition, she is a psychotherapist who has worked for many years with survivors of abuse and trauma. Her author website is www.elizabethzelvin.com.

Made in the USA
Middletown, DE
20 August 2021